Tadhg and the Pockel
by Michael Sands

For Catherine, Katie and Tóla

This is a fictional book and none of the
characters involved bear any intended
resemblance to any persons living or dead.

Published in 2017 by Shanway Press,
15 Crumlin Road, Belfast BT14 6AA

Cover design: DavidLee Badger

ISBN: 978-1-910044-13-1

About the author

Michael Sands is originally from Newry and has listened to and played folk and traditional Irish music all his life. He now teaches Irish language, guitar and banjo and runs the glens of Antrim's only bilingual B&B – *Teach an Cheoil*.

He has previously written the Celtic fantasy – Nut Hollow, the Knife and Nefairious. He followed this with two collections of poetry – Away with Words and A Moment's Notice.

He now lives in the Kingdom of Carey, outside Ballycastle, and is happily married to Catherine and is a proud father of Katie and Tóla.

Acknowledgements

This book is a thank you to each and every traditional musician and session supporter I have met along the way. I would like to thank the team at Shanway Press for travelling along with Tadhg and the boys. I would like to thank my family and friends who have supported all my writing efforts. I would like especially to thank my wife Catherine and our children Katie and Tóla who are a constant inspiration and source of all things good.

Chapters

1. Morning has broken

Tadhg – (man)   *A well intentioned civil cratur with a fondness for drink.*
Pockel – (noun)   *A bollox! A fuckin' ejit. A dose and pollution and yet... strangely likeable.*

"What sort of a blue fuck are ye? Jesus fuckin' wept!" he moaned.

Where am I?

He was afraid to open both eyes at once in case his head blew up. Right one first. A haze of grass and mud invaded and then there was the taste in his mouth. The one where the bear opens it up and shits in it.

"Ah Jesus."

He began the first of the upper body movements, still with one eye open. He was face down and his brain now slowly informed him that his hands were palms down by his sides. He pushed himself up in a way that would remind you of a fit gymnast doing that stupid running about thing with a ball. Of course he was as far from gymnast like as it was possible to be and looked like a homeless snail. His movements then were restricted as he realised he was inside a sleeping bag.

What the..?

He felt his left big toe moving inside his sock inside his boot.

Where there's life there's hope.

He decided to wiggle his toe a bit longer, in preparation if you will. It sort of kept him calm.

"Right you prick, up," he ordered.

He unzipped his container and crawled out sloth like. The early light sat on his head like an elephant. It was grey and heavy and the trunk of a hangover smacked him full in the face. Tadhg's eyes were as red as a slapped arse on a frosty morning along Newry canal and his breath stunk like a labourer's alcoholic sock.

Christ, what happened?

It was one of those rogue thoughts he didn't want to acknowledge because if he found the answer it would lead to a barrel of shit.

The surrounds now were becoming familiar. He recognised that white door, the ornate stonework around each of the many windows. The grass now swirling round his mouth was well cut. The apple trees and various flowers were well mended and trimmed…he was in the garden of the Parochial House.

Oh fuck, what day is this? Both eyes now open.

"Sunday!"

"Jesus! Mass!"

2. Like the First Morning

It had been another unremarkable morning in the life of Fr Dower. He had eaten his breakfast quickly, a little micro-waved pizza with a glass of Shloer. Not the usual stuff for one of God's Soldiers right enough, but it did the job.

His sleep had been somewhat disjointed and he was running a bit late hence the zapped breakfast. He hated being late and pulled on his pitch black jacket to finish off his priestly garb.

The wooden floors creaked as he stepped lightly over them, his shoe noise cushioned under the old carpets that had been there long before him. The house was silent once again except for the ticking of the clocks in the sitting room. He had three clocks in the same room and still he was late. He wound them every morning as his last duty in the house before saying first mass and it was to this room he took himself.

The view was calmness itself even in a northern gale. His parochial abode sat a little off the road and was sheltered by many tall and willing pines. After turning the key in the third clock and closing the glass front he decided he would steal a moment and look into his slice of Heaven. The chrysanthemums which arced majestically all along the edge of the garden were just awaking from their nocturnal slumber. He gazed happily through the crisscrossed frame on his window.

"What the fuck?" he blurted.

Sorry Lord.

He hated cursing but what was the shape in front of him that had apparently ploughed up all his yellow headed wonders?

He looked quickly at his watch, two minutes to nine. Mass started at nine. It took three minutes to get to the church. What was he to do?

"May the Lord forgive me but mass will have to wait."

He crossed himself just to make sure he wouldn't be struck down.

He would vent his building fury on the creature in his garden and no mistake. He reached for his cane and gave it a swish.

"As Jesus cast them out of the temple…" he quoted with gusto.

He quickly reached the front door and in a thrice it was open. He spied the strewn figure in the distance.

"No by Heaven, not Christ's anthems," he yelled.

The distance to the protruding rump of the intruder was as close to fifty feet as to make no difference. Fr Dower kicked up his heels and was running toward it. The cane gained in altitude and he meant to bring it down with the wrath of

God. Thirty feet now and the wind gushed through his greying hairs. They would have to be carefully reapplied to his scalp after this little contretemps…more time wasted.

As he approached he heard the word 'smote' in his head.

Ah the disciples and discipline…no coincidence I'll wager.

Suddenly he was on him, the jean covered arse creature still half up, half down, half escaped from his shell covered in petals and mud.

"How dare you desecrate holy ground," he said in high urgency.

The first of the blows fell on the soft lump Tadhg had felt earlier, cushioning the blow somewhat but doing untold damage to the lump.

"Get up and face me you cur. Look at the state of this place."

Another solid swish to the right buttock, now shorn of protection.

"Owww," yelled the creature.

"Oh you may shout alright, by God," roared the normally quiet priest, raising the cane once more.

"Ah fuck me Da, would ye stop?" shouted the arse thing turning around.

"It's me! It's Tadhg!"

3. In the Interim

For many weeks afterwards the parishioners chewed over the possibility that mass that morning had been the fastest in living memory. The sexton had it unofficially timed at 17 minutes and 53 seconds. He was convinced he could tell his grand children he had been part of a world record. There was hardly as much as a handshake or a 'How are ye doing at all?' such was Fr Dower's alacrity from the altar.

"Mass is ended, go in peace to love and serve the Lord," he'd said.

What the Hell is going on?

He whisked himself through the vestry without even getting into his black attire. Several locals had their faith in banshees reignited as his long white robe billowed behind him. To be fair they had gotten used to him and he was a little odd in some ways but these days they were happy to have a priest at all. They were not overly concerned then as he scarpered back toward the Parochial House at speed in the manner of an escaped pillow case.

After the initial shock and with time of the essence he had quickly told Tadhg to get himself and his sleeping bag out of sight and for God's sake wash himself. They would deal with this later. The last of his hairs were fixed in place and he swept in just as the altar boy thought he would have to say mass.

So he returned in some dread to the front door from which all things seemed so serene just a little while before.

Had it really happened?

He put the key in the lock.

His answer lay in the mud trail, dandelion stalks and grass cuttings scattered about his hall. He also noticed a small plastic packet…

'Ribbed for extra pleasure'

"Jesus!"

He dropped the devil's plastic helper to the floor. Condoms were not a common sight in the Parochial House.

The clothes trail led him upstairs to the bathroom door where he saw the jeans he'd hit so rigorously earlier.

"What in the name of God?"

His eyes were drawn to the soft lumpy goo that adorned the middle seam at the back of the jeans. It wasn't brown. It was white with veins of blue running through it and the smell of it worse than the other stuff one might expect in that region.

Blue cheese? What is he doing with blue cheese in his trousers?

The dull lapping of a full bath hinted an answer would be found from the wearer himself. He knocked loudly on the door and got, "Wha'?" for an answer.

Then,

"I'll be out in a bit. You wouldn't do us a bacon buttie would ye? I'm dyin'."

It was still only a quarter to ten in the morning. There would be a new world in store for the priest by five past.

4. Towel…Tea

Tadhg's head was moving slowly out of the throbbing stage with any movement to the just plain ordinary sore as fuck stage. He was furiously trying to put together what happened last night. His efforts even had musical accompaniment. Tunes!

I need a Panadol sandwich.

He dried himself off.

His head continued churn out random thought after thought.

Obviously a shower man, bath's never used… and

Blue cheese in me fuckin' jeans. Jesus!

He looked in the mirror above the old white sink. The taps must've been turned a million times but he couldn't get the hot tap to go.

"For fuck's sake!"

Both hands and it turned. He began to shave the whin bush like stubble off his face. Two minutes later he looked like a dart board and stuck on several bits of toilet paper to stem the flow of his well thinned blood. He dressed himself in one of the robes that hung behind the door. His clothes were bogging and wet and he would ask could he put them in the wash. He opened the door and looked down the stairs, no sign of father.

"Do you take sugar?"

Ah life saver.

"Aye please. One."

He went downstairs and looked at the priestly pictures hung down the wall. "Class of 56," he mumbled.

No, don't recognise any of them. Sure how the fuck would ye?

"Class of 57. No, not one. Where is that anyway? Lourdes or somewhere probably," he said aloud.

"No not Lourdes, although I've been many times. That's the outside of my old Seminary, just outside Banbridge," answered Fr Dower, standing at the bottom of the stairs with two steaming teas.

"How're you feeling now?" he asked.

"I hope I didn't hurt you? It's just those flowers have taken me an age to get to bloom. I shouldn't have hit you at all, I'm sorry. I've been under pressure, but still, it's no excuse."

Tadhg took the cup.

"Rough as a dog's arse. You've a fair swing on ye alright," he grinned rubbing his behind, feigning injury.

He followed the priest into the sitting room and immediately the ticking clocks began to seep into his brain. He would have to put with it though, the priest was looking answers.

"I surmised by your tone that your reference to me as 'Da' was more than the normal priestly meaning of father," began Fr Dower, a little unwillingly.

He wasn't all that sure that the answers he got would do him any good and he had irritable bowels too which flared up at all and any stressful occasions.

Tadhg was chewing his first mouthful of life saving bacon buttie and the priest would have to hold on. He sucked on each salty morsel and it felt like the bear's previous damage had been wondrously undone. He washed his mouth with a drop of the tea and although he could've been doing with going to bed he readied himself to speak.

5. Filling in the Gaps

The priest set his cup down in the saucer. He had clearly done it before and often. It didn't make a sound. The armchair in which he sat fitted him perfectly too and he began.

"Tell me Tadhg, what is going on?"

It can't be him.

"Well father," began Tadhg, the meaning of the word not lost on either of them.

"I was playing a few tunes last night in Belfast..."

"Tunes?" interrupted the priest. "You're a musician?"

"Aye, trad head."

"I see," said the priest.

He too had a penchant for the fiddle and indeed had represented his parish in scórs and fleadhs many years ago.

"What instrument?"

"Fiddle."

Shit. It might be.

"That's very good," he said. "Go on."

"Well we do this weekly session on a Saturday in the Garrick Bar, in town, you know and as usual there were plenty of pints and whatever to be had. So, me bein' me got tore into them and all of a sudden it was nine o' clock. Well if you ever played in a session..."

"Oh I did once or twice," said Fr Dower knowingly.

" ...well you'll know it can be hard to stop the...the vibe like...you know?"

"Hmm," he nodded in agreement.

"Well I dunno who suggested it but someone said there was a session happening in The House of McDonnell Bar, in Ballycastle and they were leaving and who was coming? I got my fiddle packed up and in two minutes we were on the M2 heading up the road."

"We?"

"Aye, there were six of us...Ogee, O'Malaigh, McLynn, O'Connell and Bunz and me all squeezed into an oul Ford Mondeo lashing back the Buckfast like nobody's breakfast."

"And the driver? He lashed too?"

"Who Bunz? No he wasn't drinkin'. No, doesn't drink n' drive. He just had a wee smoke en route, you know?"

"I'm sure, go on."

"Right, we landed in a wee pub on the main street there. Deadly wee spot. I remember doin' a few gigs in Oslo or somewhere and they had a 'plastic Paddy' pub with drink stains painted on the walls like, for atmosphere. Well these walls are real and ye can't clean this stuff off. It's years of craic, you know. Jokes, yarns, tantrums, tears, history, music and smoke all burnt into the place and these walls have more character than any of these new fangled bars any day…fuckin' TV's and Juke Boxes and shit everywhere."

Tadhg paused for another munch of his buttie. It was working and he felt he was coming round a bit.

"I think it's about four hundred years old and well it just makes you want to play tunes and drink Guinness, which is kinda where it gets a bit hazy. You see O'Malaigh is a hallion for the whiskey, pardon my French, but he is. Of course McLynn would drink it out of a dirty welly boot and soon enough there were six Jamieson's just looking all nectary sayin' 'drink me, drink me."

"Tadhg this all sounds like great craic but you called me 'Da'! Now why would you do something like that?" asked Fr Dower, his patience a little stretched.

"Aye well, I was just getting to it. You see that's when thon fuckin' pockel landed in."

6. The Pockel

Last night…

He had a set of hands on him that could squeeze a donkey's ballbag like a pimple. The fingers were like badly made sausages about to burst although miraculously, he had a gold ring on each one. There was enough growth under the fingernails for a drill of baby spuds and the hairs on his hands could've been plaited with ease.

He just about fitted into the split front door but had to enter sideways to be sure. He was a one-man football match…crowd n' all. "Pint," he ordered.

After the obligatory wait for the black gold that is Guinness to settle, he picked up the glass it looked like a thimble in his grasp. Two slugs later and it was gone.

"Pint," he ordered again.

This was of little concern to the barman and owner of the premises. Tom O'Neill had seen his like before and had ejected as many like him as had his good lady wife, Eileen. She, as a former teacher, still maintained the ability to reduce a grown man to a small boy with a firmly placed corrective sentence. Happily this skill was rarely required and, as she would say, 'would treat you like a gentleman until you proved you weren't one.' They were a warm and welcoming team. Nobody fucked about in Tom's, simple as that.

His presence was more tolerated than enjoyed but it was his habit to leave after three pints at the most. He had an unwritten agreement with Tom to this effect and it suited each party. Like many another from Belfast he had a summer home in Ballycastle. In fact parts of this holiday town had been given Belfast nicknames like Twinbrook on Sea or Costa del Poleglass. There was a rumour afoot that he had 'done time' for various things and 'been involved'. Whatever the truth of it he hadn't that many friends in the locale. He was harmless really and his own worst enemy.

The creamy foam of well hung Guinness clung to the sides of his glass until they succumbed to a deep inhale and were gone. Two down. "Pint," he said again.

He only now looked around the bar, the strains of traditional music pricking his interest. In the confined spaces of the busy pub his movement toward the music was akin to the Exxon Valdez negotiating an Alaskan Bay only with a lot less water to work with. There were noses against pint glasses, dents in toes and many bodily areas got inappropriate fondles albeit accidental ones. On he lumbered through the second doorway that split the old bar until he stood like an eclipse at the musicians' table.

"Well we all stopped and looked at him, didn't know what to expect, you know," continued Tadhg.

"Next thing you know he looks at me and says 'wee word' and kinda tried to usher me out with a nod or two. I near broke me arse laughing 'cos here's this fella the size of the fuckin' Black Mountain and he sounds like a wee girl. Sort of Belfast thing you know?"

Fr Dower sipped a little more of his tea and nodded. He wasn't one for such generalisations but had met a few Belfast men with voices that seemed to have unbroken themselves.

"Well apart from the size of him I didn't really pass any remarks and turned away again. Bunz lit up a few reels on the banjo and I thought nothing more about him. Once we had finished the set of tunes it was my turn to take the fresh air out of the pint glasses and headed for the bar. Wasn't yer man still there?"

"Wee word…nye!" he said.

"Well what harm could it do?" I thought and we went out the back where the smokers were.

"What's the craic big man?" says me.

"I'm gonna keep this short and sweet," he says. "Turns out me and you are sorta related and your Da is the local priest out the road."

Well I just looked at him and then the big shite gives me this bear hug and nearly breaks all me fucking ribs. Jesus, no wonder I'm sore the day."

Fr Dower put up his hand and dropped the cup from the other. Now it seemed he had inherited a whole family in the last five minutes. He felt altogether not right and stood up and walked to the mantelpiece. He picked up a poker and gave the grate a clear out. He bent down and in no time had the fire crackling up the chimney.

"So Tadhg if there is any truth in this, and frankly I'm becoming more doubtful by the minute, who and where is your mother?"

Couldn't be?

"Aye well that is the complicated bit. You see she died about three months ago but in her will she left me this," he answered.

From his jacket, which the priest had hung up earlier he took out a wallet and removed a small passport sized photo and gave it to Fr Dower.

"Oh my Lord," said the priest.

The small print portrayed a loving couple, him a good bit older than her but both looking devotedly into each other's eyes.

"It's Maggie," he whispered.

"Aye that's me Ma."

7. The Priest's Tale

The priest's tea left a small brown stain just where it had splashed onto the well worn beige carpet. The impossibly small little flowery cup lay awkwardly on its side in need of rescue. Tadhg would have lifted it but he was finding it hard to lift his head never mind anything else. Fr Dower stepped away from the fire picked up the cup precisely with finger and thumb and sat down again.

"Maggie Downey," he said just in a breath.

"Maggie Downey, my goodness me…"

"Aye that's Mummy eh? Full of surprises it seems," said Tadhg, happy that the spotlight had been turned off him for a while.

The bacon buttie was proving only a temporary respite and Tadhg felt himself wilt suddenly due the lack of sleep and the avalanche of slurp from last night.

"Here Father, ye wouldn't have a wee drop of something you know, to keep me goin'?"

"There's coffee?" said the priest.

"No, not coffee Father. Something with a bit of a ding, you know?"

In normal circumstances Fr Dower would not have approved of such early imbibing but these were not normal circumstances.

"You'll find some Jamieson's in the cupboard there," he said pointing to an old two door wooden drinks cabinet.

"Oh Christ no. Sorry Father, maybe a beer or something. Fuck if I have another Jamieson I'll be snottered in no time."

"Have a look. There should be something," replied the priest.

"So your Mummy is dead?" he asked as Tadhg snapped the lid off a pint bottle of Harp.

"Aye she is.

"I'm sorry to hear that."

She's buried down in Mayobridge just outside Newry, you know it?" asked Tadhg.

"I do indeed; I played football against the 'Bridge many's a time. I studied in 'In Nomine Patri et Fili' Seminary you see, to be a missionary. It's just outside Banbridge. I was going to go to off and do my bit."

"Oh and I presume it was round this time you met me Ma?" said Tadhg after a good long slug of the cure.

"It was indeed," said the priest, smiling.

"She was a cleaning lady. 'In Nomine Patri et Fili' is a huge place and they're quite keen that everything is spick and span, so each morning a gang of them would come in from Newry and give it the once over. I was just coming from morning ablutions when I saw her. Now this doesn't sound right coming from a priest but the first sight I got of her was her backside. She was cleaning the floor you see. Well I decided right then I'd have to go back to confessions for another few decades of the Rosary."

"Ha! You dirty oul' fucker. Is that what they mean by the missionary position?" laughed Tadhg.

Fr Dower grinned; he was a man after all.

"When she did turn around we got talking and it was all very bland and harmless of course but then she sort reached out and touched my hand and didn't my heart beat like mad. She had the loveliest smile. We would see each other regularly in the halls there and we became very friendly."

"Must a' been," said Tadhg cheekily.

"It was all above board. Any carry on was a no-no those times but deep down I suppose we knew there was something."

Tadhg took another good dram of the Harp. The fizz of it shot straight from the back of his throat and out his nose.

"Oh fuck! Down the wrong road."

He spluttered about on the chair but put his hand up to say 'I'm grand, go on'.

Fr Dower inhaled and continued. .

8. The Truth Will Out

Thirty two years ago…

"We probably should stop things right here," said Fr Dower, who was just Eugene to Maggie.

"But we haven't done anything wrong," she answered.

"I know but this is all a bit confusing, you know. I'm meant to be beyond all these feelings," he said.

They were well out of sight on the vast grounds of 'In Nomine Patri et Fili' College. The sun was edging slowly toward the horizon and the flies were hanging lazily above the lake. It was a scenic spot often used for weddings and in the distance they could hear the laughter and clink of glasses of just such a photo shoot. The path on which they walked was submerged in the broken branched light of early evening and it was warm enough for short sleeves.

"Your ladies will be finishing up soon, we'd better head back," said Eugene.

They had walked together a few times now but never as much as hand in hand, until now. Maggie walked ahead of him until he had to stop and kissed him.

"Thanks for listening," she said.

They were just in sight of the main house and there wasn't time for Eugene to reciprocate. He pulled out the bible from his inner coat pocket and to all eyes that may have seen them they looked like student and teacher in conversation.

"So my Ma kissed you eh?" said Tadhg suddenly. "Fair play to her."

"She did indeed and that was the start of it," he answered.

"We would meet whenever we could around the grounds and it was all very innocent believe me, but it got a bit more serious fairly soon after. I had a conference on the Need for Celibacy would you believe in Dublin and was staying in a wee B&B off Grafton Street. I had my own room and to be honest I was beginning to weaken to the temptations of the flesh."

"The conference didn't work then," quipped Tadhg, now happily half way down the bottle.

"No it certainly did not. If I said it was a torrid weekend I believe I'd be saying enough."

"Ha, ye would indeed. I get the picture," answered Tadhg.

"Yes well, there was that great sense of freedom in Dublin you know. We could be ourselves. I could dress normally and we didn't cause a second glance. But that was maybe the trouble because our real worlds waited back in and around the seminary. We did travel to a few music festivals I recall but things weren't the same."

"So ye dumped her?" asked Tadhg sitting up.

"No, quite the opposite. Your Mum pulled the pin. I think she knew that I was destined for a single life. We loved each other passionately but knew that we could never repeat those passions again."

"The damage was done though?" asked Tadhg.

"If you are referring to yourself, then yes your Mum fell pregnant after that."

"So I'm a fuckin' Mexican," gasped Tadhg.

"A what?"

"You know, south of the border…down Mexico way?"

"Oh I see. Well you could consider yourself a Dub from that point of view," answered the priest.

"A Dub! Your hole. Sorry father, but cut me and I bleed red and black. An Dún abú."

"I'm an Armagh man myself," said Fr Dower.

"Bollox! Jesus yiz are hard to listen to," quipped Tadhg, smiling.

This was not the time for a debate on the merits of one of Ulster Football's great rivalries.

"So what happened then? I mean I take it you knew she was up the du-… pregnant?"

"I knew but not right away. In fact it was a couple years later when I got this."

9. Thirst

"Ha, the fuckin' head on me," exclaimed Tadhg, gazing at the little black and white picture of himself.

"I must've have only been about what…two?"

"Aye, about that and I never thought I'd ever see the grown up version," answered Fr Dower.

"So what happened when the big guy set you down last night?" asked Fr Dower.

A little verbal tennis the order of the day.

Your serve, Tadhg.

"Oh aye right enough, I never got finishing that," he answered.

"Well of course I told yer man to catch a fuckin' grip. Cousins? Fuck sake, Obama and Osama are closer relatives. But he was havin' none of it."

"Look our fella," he says, "I've been waitin' a long time to meet you. Turns out my Da was married to your Ma's cousin or somethin'.

Hardly family.

"Anyway brother," he says. "I've got to tell about what happened your Mum and the will and all. She left you a wack a dough you know."

"Well suddenly his story became a lot more interestin' and we went back inside. I let the lads play away and me and himself went up to the bar. He had his Guinness and I ordered seven whiskeys?"

"Seven?" asked the priest.

"Fuckin' right. I needed two after that news."

"So the big lad tells me that my Ma died peacefully a few months ago."

"You didn't know she'd died?" asked Fr Dower.

"No. I hadn't seen her for a long time. Ach it's all a bit messy really and the worst of it was we didn't have a big mad row or anything like that. I hit the road when I was about twenty and never really came home again. I would ring her the odd time but we just drifted apart and it got harder and harder to call in. I know I should've tried more often but you know how it is. Anyway, if you can't get pissed when you're Ma dies…you know," said Tadhg, en route to the drinks cabinet.

"I'm gonna get another one ok?"

"Yes surely, work away."

"Well, after a good few years on the road…Australia, Russia, New Zealand, me and the fiddle of course, I came home. It was time to get back and make a go of it. So after dossin' on friends' couches for a while I got a wee flat off the Ormeau Road in the city, Fitzroy Avenue. Just the job you know. I got to know the local musos and started playin' a few sessions. They're some players I'm tellin' ye. I had a wee delivery job and was ready funny enough to go and see mum. But then didn't yer man land into Tom's with the news. He says that the will was read and her possessions were given away to charity. Turns out she had been pretty savvy with her money. So the big lad whose name I think was Terry or Robbie…Paddy maybe, finishes his pint and tells me he'll meet me back in Tom's today at one and that all I had to do was contact you and you'd know what to do. I didn't intend to contact you just so…like this you know."

"Me?" exclaimed the priest, ignoring Tadhg's half apology.

The thought that his secret was not so secret caused him great concern.

"You mean others know about me and your mum and you?"

"Well as far as I know 'tis just thon big pockel and us," answered Tadhg, with his second bottle at the giving angle.

"So we have to meet him today at one in Tom's?" said Fr Dower.

"Yep."

"But I don't see how I…I mean I don't know…I mean I have to visit people," spluttered the priest.

"Well Dad, the only visitin' you'll be doin' today will be to the tavern with me."

10. Opening Time

Tadhg's clothes were now dry.

"Tumble dryers eh? Great yokes," he said, as he pulled them out.

He'd had a doze after the second bottle and felt a lot better for it. Fr Dower had tended to a few priestly concerns and made a few apologetic phone calls to expectant parishioners.

"Mrs McLean makes the most lovely pot roast you know Tadhg," he said mournfully.

No roast today.

The three clocks on the mantelpiece had now ticked their way around to twelve thirty. It was time to head for the town. Tadhg picked up his mobile phone off the mantelpiece and pressed a few buttons.

"Bunz, ye bollox. What's the craic?"

Fr Dower heard the usual 'umms and ayes' that short phone calls demand.

"Wait 'til I get that fucker. Blue cheese! He'll be sucking it through a straw... aye but how the fuck did I get here?

Oh right...taxi...Glenview Arms...party...holiday cottages...he ended up with yer one...asleep on the fuckin' loo! Jesus...oh right, it took two of yiz to carry me...sleepin' bag...meant to come back...forgot. What do ya mean I woke ye up? I'm in the priest's fuckin' parlour. Aye...ok...Tom's...two-ish...I'll see yiz there, g'luck."

Fr Dower opened the door and went to the car. Tadhg followed and looked guiltily at the chrysanthemum corpses scattered about the place.

"Here, I'll throw you a few poun' for them flowers, ok?" he offered.

"Hmmm, put some money in the collection tray next time eh," answered the priest.

"Aye, grand."

Unlikely.

Fr Dower headed out the gate toward the town. He drove an Avensis, a recent model too.

"Nice wagon, Father," commented Tadhg, smoothing his fingers over the upholstery.

"You boys always seem to get a nice car."

"Well we do cover a lot of ground and it's not really ours, it belongs to the parish," answered Fr Dower.

Tadhg had an 'aye fuckin' right' on the tip of his tongue.

The drive down into Ballycastle is a joy. On the right hand side you see

Scotland, Rathlin Island and Kenbane Head all showing off under the often changing sky. On the left is the intimidating presence of Knock Layde, most of the time with its head in the clouds. Then there were the foothills and as they say, Antrim's hills so blue. Yellow whin bushes, sycamores and as many birds as you could wish for scattering themselves about the telephone wires and beyond. The long hill into town rolled gracefully before them. A few deft turns of the steering wheel and they were soon in the 'Diamond' car park just down from Tom's. Sundays in Ballycastle brought out the crowds and today with the sun and all there was a good vibe going round.

"Fuck I could murder a pint," said Tadhg.

"Tadhg, you might want to lay off the curse words just a bit, you know, just in company," said the priest.

"Aye ok Father, sorry. Bad habit."

They got out of the car and into the afternoon and strolled the short distance to The House of McDonnell. As ever it took a moment to adjust to the darkness of inside but quickly they could see they were the first in. Each stood at the counter and Tom was quickly there to take an order.

"Pint of Guinness please, Tom," began Tadhg. "It'll either cure me or kill me."

"And Father Dower we don't often see you in here. What'll you have?"

"Ah I know Tom but you never know what's in store do you? Eh...I'll just have a sparkling water please with lime."

Tom went off to the Guinness taps and the hiss of stout brought a sigh of contentment from Tadhg. He leaned on the counter, and studied briefly its many contours, he felt better already. This ancient wooden bar had housed a million elbows and its varnish had yielded in places to their pressing. It had heard the same amount in yarns. The equally ready four legged wooden stools lined up soldier like below. Manys the backside had found relief and rescue on them. Suddenly the glass door of the front doors was cast in shadow. The Pockel was right on time.

11. Directions

"Pint," he ordered, before even acknowledging the others.

Tom had the glass in his hand before he got to 't'.

"Right," he began, "down the back, nye."

The three of them moved to a small round room that sat just off the main bar area like a confessional chamber. In fact all that was missing were a few holy pictures and a curtain. The Pockel's bulk made it a tight squeeze but they managed each to find a space.

"Before you begin," said Fr Dower, "would you mind if I asked you what your name is?"

"No I don't mind but it makes no odds. Just call me Pete."

Ha fuckin' priceless, thought Tadhg. *Pete the Pockel.*

His smile was quickly hidden in the froth of his pint for fear of a slap in the teeth. He had no cause for concern though.

"Well," said Pete, "I'm sure you are both wondering what's goin' on? Aye, well me too. Hopefully this'll help."

From his Denim jacket, not unlike a blue balloon wrapped around an over sized spud, he pulled out a small white envelope. He placed it on the table.

FAO Tadhg Downey ONLY

"Would you like a moment alone Tadhg?" asked Fr Dower.

"Ach, no it's alright," he replied picking up the envelope.

Pete had headed for the bar again.

"Pint."

He looked at Tom and pointed to the other two as if to say 'same again' for them. Tom being the ever alert barman had sussed the others were not ready just yet and contented himself with Pete's Guinness. Rarely did pints get such attention as they did from Tom. He handled the glass as if handling a rare egg and spun it as the liquid entered. The silent settling of the stout was punctuated with little taps from an antique steel knife, some say dated from the table of Sorley 'boy' McDonnell. As the pint fulfilled its gaseous requirements Tadhg ripped open the little envelope and held the folded letter in his hand.

"Here goes."

Pete returned and sat down just as Tadhg began to read.

Dear son,

I hope this finds you well. I'm sorry to say that if you are reading this we didn't meet up again and I am dead. It feels a bit funny to write that, perhaps odd to read too?

No shit.

Over the years I came to realise that we were never destined to be very close although I always thought about you and wondered how you were getting on. I worked here and there and it was ok. Anyway I have saved up £15,000.00 more or less and would like you to have it.

Stickin' fuckin' out!

It's in a bank account and I was just going to leave you the account number but thought well, there's no fun in that. I know you loved to travel and so I have a little challenge for you. Do you still play the fiddle? I hope so…here's why.

"Tom, do us a wee Jemmie will ye?" shouted Tadhg, suddenly in need of a shot of something strong.

All being well you should be sitting beside Pete and your father. Ask your father for the photograph of you again.

"Oh, right ok. Father you wouldn't show us that we picture of me again would ye?"

"Of course," replied Fr Dower.

Please examine the photo carefully.

Tadhg picked up the photo and looked at it. It was just a picture of a toddler as far as he could see.

If you notice the t-shirt you are wearing in the picture you will see it says Baltimore 1980. This is reference to the Cork Fleadh that was held there that year. Now that was the year I entered my one and only Fleadh…on the fiddle. I lived down there for a year or three and met some wonderful people. Anyway there is a small pub in the centre of town called McCarthy's where each year now they have a fiddle music festival. Your first clue is there…ask for Mick the Flick.

Good luck son, I know you'll find it. You may take whomever you please with you but you must include Pete, he's a bit…well you'll see. He's a good man.

Love and kisses, Mum.

12. Let the Games Begin

"Ha! She must've been off her fuckin' head when she wrote this," exclaimed Tadhg.

"What did it say?" asked Fr Dower, more interested than he realised.

"I have to go to Cork, Baltimore to be exact and ask for Mick the Flick in McCarthy's pub. Does this ring any bells Father?"

"Mick the Flick! I don't believe it," gasped the priest.

"Mick the who?" asked Pete.

"Mick Culane. He was a really good friend of your mum's, played fiddle. He wouldn't remember me I'm sure. I often wondered how he'd ended up," answered Fr Dower.

"Right lads," said Tadhg, "it's no bother for me to head down apart from havin' no car and fuck all dough but she says Pete you have to come."

"Aye don't worry captain, I'm with ye," said Pete.

"That just leaves yourself Father, what about it?"

Fr Dower set down his glass. He had finished it in one gulp on hearing the contents of the letter.

"Mick the Flick…Baltimore…it's all very tempting Tadhg but I've got the parish work and daily mass and any number of things to be doing. Believe me I'd love to go with you but –"

"But my arse, Father," interrupted Tadhg. "You meet your son for the first time. We have a chance to head off together and get a few quid and you're talking about visiting some oul' doll up the road. C'mon, live a bit ye boy ye. God knows you'll hardly get a chance like this again."

"Why is he called Mick the Flick?" asked Pete suddenly.

"Ach Tadhg it would be too awkward. I mean I can't just skip mass you know. That's my bread and butter. The bishop would take a dim view of it not to mention those ever present locals. They're good people. Mass gives them something to get up for, believe it or not."

"Fuck me," said Tadhg.

If mass was all I ever had to get up for I'd fuckin' shoot myself.

"Ring in sick. Sure what would they do if ye had the flu or something?"

"No Tadhg. This job is all day every day. By the way, priests don't get sick, they just die. However, as we are in the merry month of May I do have a few days holidays booked over from last year. Fr Boyle said he would stand in for me if I ever took a notion so theoretically I could follow you pair down on Wednesday. I really would like you to get your money Tadhg."

"That's fate. Tom, three drinks please," ordered Tadhg.

"Here, I'll have one too," came a voice suddenly "…and me…one here...aye it's your round ye balloon."

The musicians had landed back. Within a moment or two Tom's had filled with varying levels of expletives, curses and laughter.

"You were doing a bit of weeding I see. Will you stay for a tune Father?" asked Bunz, who had poked his head into the little snug to see the three in conference.

Weeding? Ah yes, Tadhg!

"Your friends? Ah, now sure I'll just listen awhile," he answered.

"I'd say the lads are feeling worse than you by the looks of them," whispered the priest.

"Ach now Father it's a trad thing, slap it up 'em. No Surrender, know what I mean?" laughed Tadhg.

Soon strings were tuned and bows got rosined. Ogee hit the bodhrán a few taps and the potential for bedlam had been stirred.

"Oh and Pete…" said Fr Dower, "he's called Mick the Flick because of his dexterity with the bow. They say he can kill a fly without missing a note."

"Aye, dead on. Wax on-wax off Grasshopper," replied Pete.

The illicit mixture of daylight, beer, tunes and a generous barman soon had its effect. The tunes were bouncing around the pub without hindrance. Whatever ailments last night's excesses had delivered were quickly overcome. Word spread and the pub began to fill again. There were several glances at Pete and some small talk but he was no musician as far as anyone knew and remained in the little room alone peering out as Fr Dower and Tadhg joined the circle just beyond. He did seem to enjoy the tunes though and for now that would do.

13. Another Note or Two

It quickly became clear to Fr Dower that the bums were well settled on the seats. There was no let up in the supply of pints and the session was picking up speed. He felt it may be an opportune time to remind Tadhg that while he was welcome to stay the night he would rather he slept inside the house. However, in the melee of energy and insanity that a good session is, wisdom falls like an autumn leaf and is often ignored.

"Tadhg, I have to go now. If you don't go back to Belfast tonight come out and you can start afresh tomorrow."

"Ah give us a tune Father before you go," asked O'Connell.

O'Connell was quite well built, for a musician. His brown hair was reduced to a mere shadow on his head. In recent years he had taken to long distance cycling, much to Tadhg's bafflement. Today though, no bikes were looked for. He held his bouzouki in readiness.

"Here's me fiddle," offered Tadhg quickly not wishing to burst the session buzz with sense and reality.

Fr Dower hadn't picked up a fiddle for some time and the moment or two he took to think about accepting the offer was taken as a yes.

"Quiet please, quiet," shouted Ogee. "A tune from the priest."

"Here," says McLynn, "this'll do for mass. Me Ma'll be thrilled."

Fr Dower felt a bit awkward. He was handling someone else's instrument. There was that element of the unknown about it even though it was the one he knew. He cradled the fiddle baby like and ran his thumb quickly over the four strings. Their stubbed short response told him each was in tune.

"Right," he said, "give me a hand out here lads…it's been a while."

He raised the bow of the fiddle up under his chin. He'd done it before. The bow he brought up onto the first string and as nice as ninepence he began with a jig. His feet were his first accompaniment, tapping and tip toeing in time. Other feet followed.

"That's The Butterfly," whispered Bunz and immediately he followed in behind on the banjo.

Next came the exotic tones of O'Connell's bouzouki and then Ogee's drum. The rust was soon shaken from Fr Dower's arm and off he went into another tune to a loud 'hup' from McLynn, joining in another fiddle.

"Go on Father, lovely stuff," said Tadhg.

Pete tapped his toes. He was getting into the swing of things.

Not bad.

"Pint."

This was his third and therefore he too would be leaving soon. Tom left his drink at the bar and took a few photos of the impromptu gathering for his gallery like walls.

Fr Dower finished off his set to much yahooing and clapping.

"That brings me back," he said smiling.

"Now Father you'll play us another one. Sure a bird never flew on one wing," said Bunz.

Fr Dower refused gracefully, returned the fiddle, said his thank-yous and goodbyes and left. He had only stood up when as if to play him out the lads all started another wave of tunes.

Here we go, thought Tadhg, *sex, drugs and diddly dee.*

He felt the skin behind his ears tighten and a general fuzz in his head. Pete leaned over and whispered into Tadhg's ear.

"Look I've gotta go after this one and it looks like you could be here for a while. I'm gonna drive you to Baltimore but we're hittin' the road early, got it. It's a nine hour spin you know. Give me your mobile number and I'll text you at eightish the marra mornin' ok?"

"Aye no bother," answered Tadhg, suddenly with a carte blanche to get pissed.

The two exchanged numbers and Pete polished off his pint in a single slug and left. The almost clandestine nature of their interaction brought a curious look or two from the troupe.

"Who the fuck's yer man?" asked O'Connell.

"Aye what's the craic? You get yourself a bouncer or what?" asked O'Malaigh, who had just bought the first of the Jamiesons.

"Here, it's a long story. It's all good...somebody play a tune."

14. The Return of the Pockel

O'Malaigh saw him first although he could not quite believe what filled his view. The opaque almost jaundiced windows of Tom's front door disguised the flesh coloured blob until they were forced open. Several hours had passed and there was a definite slackening off of pace so much so that several songs had been allowed. However, this did not prepare the gathering for what the wind blew in.

Standing now at the front door without as much as a sock on was the Pockel. Not only that but he had the brass balls to walk up to Eileen, Tom's good lady wife, behind the bar and say, "Pint!"

Tom had grabbed a coat off the wall behind him but even he was not quick enough. With the dexterity of a ballet dancer the big lad skipped down through the bar, his bits bouncing in time and stood once more at the circle of musicians.

"Da Daaaa! 'Tis I. Bruce of the Forsythes and for your pleasure I will dance the Kerry Set," he yelled and up onto his tip toes he got.

Tom was not going to miss him a second time. A long time rugby fan he had been buoyed up no end with Ireland's recent triumph in the Six Nations Championship. With coat at the ready he took off at the midriff of the man tank like a bespectacled matador. A man of some years, Tom's athleticism belied his age. He hit Pete just below the belly button and to avoid any awkwardness brought his fist up through the coat so that he hit Pete's swinging paraphernalia like Muhammad Ali, of whom he was also a fan. Pete hit the deck like a collapsing blancmange and squealed in agony as his testicles moved swiftly up into his stomach. He writhed about for a few moments and as if the sober fairy had landed on him he stood up rather sheepishly clinging onto the coat.

"Ye big gulpin! Out!" roared Tom, with the musicians and half the bar standing shoulder to shoulder behind him.

"You're barred for life and if ye die you're barred for death too."

Pete was ushered out onto the street by many hands and eyes.

"Here, that's your new mate Tadhg. You'd better sort him out," said O'Malaigh, sliding his hand round his glass as the mood calmed again.

"Fuck me," sighed Tadhg.

He set down his fiddle and went outside to see Pete picking up his clothes off the street. The locals in the chip shop cancelled their orders for battered sausages on seeing the naked oaf lumber past the window.

"What the fuck was that all about? Bruce of the Forsythes?" gasped Tadhg.

He had managed to steer him down an alley way where he was now redressing himself.

"Hang loose, I'll be back in a deuce! It'll be a big night if ye play your cards right. Sure I didn't mean any harm," replied Pete, breathing heavily down his nose.

"Harm? Fuck sake you walked into Tom's bollox naked you dose. What did you think would happen? Christ! C'mon everybody strip and do the fuckin' Kerry Set," said Tadhg, now suddenly a beacon of wisdom.

Pete slowly buttoned up his shirt. He now looked as he did before but his eyes were still swimming about in his head.

"Time you were home big man," said Tadhg.

They walked down to the taxi rank and Pete got in.

"Right I'll wait for your call tomorrow ok? Perhaps it'll be a bit after eight, the fuckin' state of ye," said Tadhg not accustomed to being the good Samaritan.

"Aye yer hole," huffed Pete and closed the door.

Tadhg watched the taxi head up the hill toward the housing estate high on the hill above the town. God only knew what tomorrow held in store but for now tomorrow could wait.

15. Decisions, decisions

"That's the sort of thing that happens after the third pint," said Tom.

"He must've got carried away with the music and all for it must be…oh…five years since he's done anything like that."

"So he's got form?" said Tadhg.

"Put it this way, how would you feel if he jumped up onto your table and began Riverdance?" said Tom shaking his head, the memory obviously seared into his mind.

"Riverdance? Him?" said Tadhg.

"Yes, he's not exactly Flatley is he?" replied Tom.

"There was carnage. Table broken of course and drink hanging off the rafters but thankfully no fatalities. He did apologise the next day and we came to a 'three pints and you're gone' agreement. It would seem he's had three pints in every other bloody pub in the town today."

Tom had seen many things in his day in the bar and was well equipped to deal with them. He was by no means tall or particularly well built but he was tight. There was no spare flesh on his bones but he had been used to shifting beer kegs most of his adult life. As he had proved he could handle himself but perhaps more importantly he had the respect of his punters and his was the best pub in Ballycastle.

"Right Tom, give them hallions a round," said Tadhg and rejoined the band.

"Well did you get Bruce sorted out?" asked McLynn.

"Aye, silly big fucker's away up the road in a joey."

He was not sure just exactly how to play this. Should he disclose all about the will and the Baltimore trip? He didn't dwell long on it.

"What a day. You remember you bastards left me in the priest's garden last night?"

Much smirking.

"Well turns out I have to head to Baltimore in the morning. Twinkle Toes himself is gonna drive me too. Anybody up for a spin to Cork?"

This would do for now. They didn't need to know all. He could say he was a family friend or something if they even bothered to ask.

"Baltimore!" said Ogee. "What date is this?"

"Sixth of May, why?" replied O'Malaigh looking at his watch.

"For a start the Fiddle Fair starts on the seventh and I do not have to get up for work in the morning, so if there's room Tadhg I'm with ye," replied Ogee giving his long black hair a comb back with his fingers.

Ogee didn't have to get up for work any morning. He worked at night with a variety of bands. He was a drum for hire and a lover of life, liquor and ladies.

"One down, what about it Bunz?" asked Tadhg.

"Are you soft in the fuckin' head? Did you forget my three wains? I don't think Olive'd be thrilled if I told her I was for Cork after this weekend. No, I doubt I'll be goin'."

"Fair enough sure you're workin' anyway," said Tadhg.

"Fuck aye, don't remind me," replied Bunz.

The gang all respected Bunz. Not only was he one of the best banjo players in the country, he was good natured and wickedly humoured. He had been married a while now and his attentions had shifted. His family came first.

"What about the rest of yiz?"

This was the moment in their day when on being asked a question like that the split in the road suddenly appears. The choices are often not overly contemplated upon, especially where drink has been enjoyed and a positive response will lead to more of the same. Their dilemma was the responsibility of what must be left behind for that period of absence. In their combined cases Bunz had already weighed up the options and done the right thing for the sake of his marriage. The others had to weigh up employment considerations. Well, Ogee didn't and he was all set.

"Ah fuck that is temptin'," began O'Malaigh but I have to see a man about the boiler the marra."

"Fuck the boiler," said Ogee. "C'mon sure the house'll be grand for a few days."

"Aye bollox, twist me arm…I'm there," smiled O'Malaigh, it wouldn't be long now until he'd be shouting for Jemmies.

O'Malaigh loved the tunes and was a martyr for the craic. He had a thing for Mary Bergin which only came out after many pints of stout. As a self employed painter and decorator he could work as he wished. Apart from the boiler the week ahead was quiet.

Two left, McLynn and O'Connell. Of all the lads time off would be most problematical for them. They both had jobs that required a fair degree of responsibility. McLynn worked for the Arts Council office, although at what exactly, no one knew. O'Connell ran the canine stud farm 'High Tails'. What he didn't know about dry humping wasn't worth knowing. They looked at each other and weighed up the pros and tried to ignore the cons.

"Well boys speak now or forever hold up the bar," said Tadhg.

"But there's no room. Fuck sake lard arse would hardly fit into a bus never mind a car," said McLynn.

"Ach we'll squeeze in and hopefully he drives a big yoke," said Ogee.

"You on?" asked McLynn.

"Aye fuck it!" answered O'Connell.

And there it was. The dogs could go fuck themselves for a day or two and sure no one would miss McLynn in the Arts Council offices anyway.

"Right Tom, drinks all round. Baltimore it is," said Tadhg.

"Hang on, hang on," said Bunz, "where ye all gonna sleep?"

16. Toilet trouble

The fairly reasonable question now sat above the company like a rain cloud.

"I'm gonna head back to Belfast now and if anybody wants to come, come on," said Bunz, searching his pockets for his keys.

"Drive?" exclaimed McLynn. "Jesus if you're stopped you're fucked. You're as drunk as the rest of us."

"I'll go the back roads."

"Back roads to Belfast? Are you off your head? You'll end up in fuckin' Portglenone or Ahoghill or somewhere. You're not driving anywhere. We'll find the big man's house and stay with him," declared Tadhg.

"What? Bruce? Sure he'll be comatose by now and no one knows where he lives," said O'Malaigh.

"The taxi man knows and he'll be back by now with any luck," said Tadhg.

It was now nearly ten at night and the energy of the day was fading as were energy levels. "Right fair enough," said O'Malaigh. "C'mon."

The lads put away their instruments and knocked back the remainders of their drinks. They put on their coats and were set to leave to try and find the Pockel's cave.

"Where the fuck's O'Connell?" asked Bunz.

As often happens, the eyes shot around the room, under the table and behind the bar. No sign. Tom's was certainly not the biggest pub to be in and quickly all possible hiding places were exhausted.

"Did he leave? He's in the chippy? Is he?" asked McLynn.

"No he didn't leave. He's still here somewhere," said Tom.

"Fucker," said O'Malaigh suddenly. "I know where he is?"

There was only one place they hadn't looked. It was known to happen that through tiredness and emotional drain the eyes become heavy and sometimes the loo is the most comfortable place to be. It's the spot for self contemplation, musings on world peace and that sort of thing. Of course a copious amount of drink is also required and all the boxes had been ticked during the afternoon.

The lads headed out and banged and shouted at the door of the toilet which sat just beyond the back door of Tom's. There was no answer. McLynn bent down and confirmed by looking under the door that indeed O'Connell was in situ, unconscious. They could have banged away all night for the good it would have done.

"I've seen this before," said Bunz. "Tom, would you have a screwdriver on you?"

Tom nodded. Of course he had. What Tom didn't keep behind the bar wasn't worth keeping. He quickly returned with said implement.

"Tom we'll replace everything as good as new but we need to take the door off," said Bunz.

Tom nodded approvingly.

So the twisting began and of course the manual labour was an opportunity to get in another round of drinks in case they would overheat. Soon enough the hinges let go their load and there he was Buddha like with his trousers and boxers around his ankles. O'Malaigh had ordered an extra pint of water.

"He'll be needing this," he said.

"Aye a drink of water will do him the world of good," said Tom.

"Sorry Tom, not this one," replied O'Malaigh and proceeded to pour the freezing water down the back of O'Connell's neck.

Never was anyone seen to move so fast about the confined quarters of a cubicle. As if suddenly jump started O'Connell stood straight up and let out a roar that sounded like a newly castrated bullock. Luckily for the onlookers his long shirt covered his gravity vulnerable mating tackle.

Thank God, thought Tom.

Two free roaming todgers in one day was enough for any man.

"Wake up ye balloon," said Tadhg.

O'Connell suddenly assumed the role of Lazarus and pulled himself together and was swiftly told that he could put the door back on. Bunz handed him the screwdriver and after minimal help they left him to it.

To a rapturous round of applause O'Connell re-entered the pub some ten minutes later.

"Fuckers!" he said, handing Tom back the screwdriver.

"That'll fuckin' learn ye?" said Tadhg, thankful for once it wasn't him in need of rescue from the porcelain pit.

Together again they headed off into the night bidding farewell to Tom, Eileen and the punters who had enjoyed the tunes.

"Right, where's that taxi?" asked Tadhg.

17. Home Sweet Home

They stumbled out onto the very hilly main street. It was all that O'Connell could do to remain vertical such was the pressure of gravity on his unsteady legs. He felt the world would stop spinning if he sat on it.

The arse knows.

"Would you get up to fuck!" shouted Bunz. "We have to find this looper's house or else we're sleeping in the fuckin' car."

"Aye c'mon there's the taxi that took him," said Tadhg.

O'Connell braced himself and stood up but kept one hand on the wall just to be sure. They made it down to the taxi and piled in the back.

"Out!" said the driver. "I only take four."

"Look mate we're just goin' up the road. Can we stick someone in the boot?" asked Tadhg.

"What? No ye fuckin' can not hi. In town you mean?" asked the driver.

"Aye, you remember that big fella I sent home with you a while ago?"

"I do aye."

"We're stayin' with him."

"Right. Ok. Squeeze in the back and pray there's no cops about."

Tadhg got the front seat and the others were jammed in place leaving the already corpse like O'Connell to lie across their laps.

"You let one go and you're gettin' fucked out the window," warned Bunz.

Of course one of the joys of Guinness is the release of black gas. Not being in control of too much at this point O'Connell felt the build up of pressure in the nether regions.

Shit, he thought. *I can't hold this.*

He would have to be careful. If he pushed too hard it could lead to the dreaded 'solid fart' and he didn't want that. With great deliberation he saved up the gas until he felt ready to burst. The release was spectacular.

"Frrriiiippppppp!!!" accompanied with a very self satisfactory laugh.

"Ah you dirty bastard," moaned the recipients in unison.

Bunz had even felt the vibration where he sat. When a toddler falls over there is usually a two or three second silence…then an explosion of noise. It was much the same with the stench. They all knew it was coming and it didn't disappoint.

"Why the fuck? I fuckin' sniffed in! Christ you're rotten," gasped Bunz.

"You shit yourself," said Tadhg, now getting the full waft in the front.

Luckily the taxi driver had his window down or else he'd have driven off the road. He looked across at Tadhg for his fee.

"Fiver'll do and get the fucker fumigated will ye? Thon's yer man's house," he said pointing.

Tadhg passed him the few pound necessary and they all got out of the car. After they had relieved the boot of their instruments they stood like that Craobh Rua CD cover in the darkness.

"Right Sherlock, where now?" asked Ogee.

"There, 16 Fairhead Gardens," answered Tadhg, leading the way.

The five stood at the front door and noticed there was a single light burning somewhere in the depths of the house.

"You reckon he's still up?" asked McLynn now bursting to get to the loo.

"Doubt it," replied Tadhg and stepped over to ring the bell.

No answer.

"Shit. Check round the back. He might have left a door open somewhere."

Ogee and McLynn headed round the back, past a big green heating oil drum and the bomb site that was his garden. They followed the light and tried the back door. It was open and in they went. Ogee took a quick scoot upstairs and found the big lad flat out fully clothed in a bedroom. McLynn let the rest in and after a quick hunt for blankets and cushions they settled themselves in for the night. Soon there was nothing to be heard but the low growl of Guinness farts and the deep inhalations of the drunk.

18. The Journey Begins

Tadhg woke first. He didn't feel a whole pile better than he did yesterday morning but at least he remembered how he'd got there. The smell in the room would have peeled the paint off a wall.

Christ the night! thought Tadhg and opened a window, carefully stepping between legs, arms and heads.

There was movement above. Tadhg hoped the big man would be in a sympathetic mood. The stairs groaned as the Pockel descended.

"I thought I heard something," he said.

"Aye only us Pete, we were kinda stuck for a kip and thought you wouldn't mind," replied Tadhg hopefully.

"Well saying as I don't remember very much after leaving Christy's bar you could maybe tell me how you knew where I lived?"

"You don't remember Tom's?" asked Tadhg.

"Oh look, Lord of the Stagger," said Bunz rolling out from underneath a coat.

"Wha'?" asked Pete with that tone only a black out can induce.

Tadhg filled him in on his exploits the night before as the rest of the strewn few woke up.

"Fuck me pink," sighed Pete, "that's me finished in Tom's."

"Aye he was a bit annoyed you might say," said Tadhg.

"What time is it?" asked Bunz, letting go a long, loud bum rush.

"Quarter past nine," answered Ogee looking all red eyed and bushy tailed.

"Shite! Here I gotta go."

"Is there room for a few more today?" Tadhg asked Pete. "What do you drive anyway?"

"One of them people carriers. An oul' Picnic," he answered.

Fate, thought Tadhg.

"Sweet," said O'Malaigh.

"Aye the more the merrier," said Pete.

"Fuck I'm starvin'," said McLynn. "Where would ye get a fry 'roun' here?"

"Aye, food," came O'Connell's voice from under his coat.

In a few moments the musketeers were dressed and ready to head out. They all clambered into the Pockel's half car, half aircraft carrier and headed into town.

"Great, the yoke's still here anyway," said Bunz.

Pete pulled up beside his car and let him out.

"Right, good luck ye shower of fuckers. You never know I might join yiz later," he said and got into the driver's seat.

Farewells were quickly shared and as were arrangements for texts and phone calls. They headed for the Thyme and Co café. Their fry ups got a swift death and all felt better for it. Time to hit the road.

The car filled up with room enough for all; Pete and Tadhg in the front, Ogee and McLynn in the middle and O'Connell and O'Malaigh at the very back. The instruments were squeezed in around feet and it wasn't too bad at all. The little green figured clock on the dashboard read ten fourteen.

"Baltimore, here we come," said Tadhg.

"How long do ya reckon then?" yawned McLynn.

"About nine hours," answered Pete, "if we don't stop that is."

"Fuck that!" exclaimed O'Malaigh. "Can we pull in at Belfast, just for one like?"

No answer from the driver, who pulled into the traffic and away up the hill out of Ballycastle.

19. A Few Lines

If his sleep the previous night was disjointed Fr Dower's sleep was virtually non-existent that night. No matter what he tried his eyelids fluttered open like roller blinds every few minutes. He had undressed himself for bed and got into his pyjamas. He didn't sleep in the buff, not now, hardly at all since Dublin all those years ago. His room was not particularly big and had basic furniture, an old fashioned wardrobe with little locks (keys still there) and a chest of drawers with a mirror on top. Below the mirror sat a white hand crochet cloth. It took his mother one month to make it for him as a gift for becoming a priest. It was rarely moved and looked delicate and ornate underneath the mirror.

He got out of bed and listened to the wind move lazily amongst the branches. He stood at the window and looked out onto the garden. The remnants of Tadhg's visit were still evident even in the near total darkness.

What a day.

He moved away from the window and switched on the little bedside lamp that sat on the chest of drawers. Its gentle creamy glow lit up his corner of the room and threw the others into doubt. Fr Dower opened the top drawer and took out his note pad and pen. He always kept a notepad handy mostly to record ideas for sermons, stuff he hoped the parishioners would find interesting. These days that was becoming more and more difficult. This night though he decided he would write a letter to a dead woman.

He found it impossible not to think about Maggie.

She was beautiful.

"Am I meant to think about women like that? Aye, you're a man first, priest second. Who invented that whole bloody celibacy thing anyway?" he wondered aloud.

He would often get into conversations with himself on any manner of topic. He picked up the pen, running it across the top of the page a few times to get the ink to flow.

Dear Maggie,
You won't believe who I met today…Tadhg, your son. Well, our son I suppose. You might say it was a bit of a shock considering I found him in the garden. Of course I didn't recognise him. I thought it was just some young lad from the town. He was a bit the worse for wear you might say. You only ever sent me one little picture. I would have

liked a few more but you had your reasons no doubt.

We got talking and here I find myself at three in the morning thinking about you like I haven't done in thirty years, explain that. I'm sure God loves me and I love him but I think I love you more, at least loved you more.

I hope you were content. You were a beautiful person when I knew you. I pray life didn't alter you as it can sometimes. Tadhg, (I like the name by the way. Irish for bard isn't it?) told me you weren't that close. I'm sorry about that. He seems a decent lad if a bit off the wall.

Maggie my darling, I don't even know why I'm writing to you but you did listen to me once and perhaps you hear me now. I've been a father in all ways except the one that counts. I think I would like to be a father or dad even, to Tadhg. Complicated you say? Yes, it surely is and I'm faced with a trip to Baltimore. Baltimore! Could ye not have picked New York? Goodness knows one's about as far away as the other.

Anyway, if you could help out I'd appreciate it. I know I should probably ask God but I never could get a bloody answer out of him. I'll probably go straight to Hell for that.

So there it is Maggie, I wish I could've seen you one more time
Love
Eugene.

20. Pit Stop

It takes about an hour and a bit to get down to Belfast from Ballycastle and by midday the yellow cranes of Harland and Woolfe stood out against the beautiful panorama that is Belfast Lough. As ever the harbour was busy with all manner of sea bound vessels going about their business. Luckily for the crew on board Pete's barge the last bit of the M2 was quiet thanks to it being a bank holiday and they avoided the relentless car broth that the working week visits upon drivers.

"What time does Madden's open?" asked O'Malaigh, now ready for anything after a snooze.

"Fair question," replied Ogee also feeling a touch thirsty.

The northern side of Belfast whizzed past their windows and it was suddenly decision time. A quick turn left onto the Falls Road and the promised land of Madden's or straight ahead…next stop Dublin.

"'S'up to you Pete," said Tadhg, "You're the driver."

"We'll stop for one," answered Pete, "I'll drop yiz off; I've a wee message to do."

"Result!" said O'Malaigh.

"See you in about a half hour," said Pete and drove off up the road.

"Ye can do a fair bit of damage in that time," smiled Ogee, "C'mon."

In spite of the sun's best efforts at keeping them they entered the dark confines of Madden's tavern. Like Tom's it was a mighty spot for traditional music and sat snugly just behind the main shopping centre. There were a few early punters in just easing into the day and O'Malaigh was quickly bar bound. Of Madden's many fine qualities the one that will catch your eye is the gallery of posters which fill just about every space on the walls that support its low ceiling; a history of music around the festivals of the country. Mixed in with these paper mementos are notices for lost dogs, lost souls and those who have nothing to lose. O'Malaigh noticed one just as the Monday Club pints began.

For sale – Fiddle, dates from 1975 approx.
In playable condition. Owner deceased.
Contact Micko – Baltimore c/o McCarthy's Tavern.

Playable? *Fuck he's hopeful*, thought O'Malaigh, now stroking his ginger stubble. "Here, there's somebody selling a fiddle from fuckin' Baltimore," he said aloud.

"Baltimore!" gasped Tadhg.

Now Tadhg didn't really go for all the usual God stuff. He was more into the late Dave Allen approach to religion of 'may your God go with you' but this coincidence got him thinking, especially as his own fiddle was nearly knackered.

"You'd think that was a sign?" said Ogee. "We were destined for Cork boys. Now get that Guinness over here, I'm starvin'."

"A sign my hole. Fuck sake, asking for Micko in Cork is like askin' for Miguel in Madrid…thousands of 'em," replied McLynn.

"Right enough but it's Baltimore. It's not Cork itself. There's a good chance we'd find him and especially if he's in McCarthy's," said Tadhg.

Several more pilgrims had found their promised land and the bar was soon waking to laughs and the craic of weekend dissection. The five pints got little mercy and Tadhg headed back up for reinforcements.

"Five more there please," he said to the barman who looked as though he too needed a cure.

"Rough night?" asked Tadhg.

"No not really. The night was fine. It's not the fall that kills ye, it's when ye hit the ground," he answered with a pained grin.

"Know what ye mean. Tunes last night I suppose?" continued Tadhg.

"Aye the usual shower of ejits and then about eleven o'clock in lands a load of ones from West Cork, from Baltimore, they said."

"Wha?" gasped Tadhg.

This was getting a bit weird.

21. Deliverance

The sun lost another pair of eyes as into the tavern strode Pete looking every bit the man mountain he was. He appeared happy enough and didn't seem bothered at the table laden with black pints. He'd had a shower.

"Fuck me," said Ogee, "you smell like a hur's handbag."

"Wind yer neck in. That's the best of aftershave you cheeky wee bollox," he snapped back.

"Did your Ma buy ye that for Christmas?" laughed O'Malaigh.

"Here, you're in no position to be givin' out…fuckin' state of yiz."

"Did you get sorted?" asked Tadhg.

"Aye just had to see a man about a dog, you know," answered Pete, this being the stock answer when you don't want to let on just what you've been doing.

"Right, fair enough. We'll get back on the road after these…ok?" said Tadhg.

"Aye, no bother. Any craic?" replied Pete.

"Aye seems there was a crowd of ones in here last night from Baltimore. What's the odds of that and us heading that road?" asked Tadhg.

"Right," said Pete, unsurprised.

They quickly had the pints nearly drunk and as ever O'Malaigh started eyeing up the top shelf.

"Right, it's time we hit dusty. Get them into yiz," said Pete, not wishing for whiskey to be added.

The pints were dispatched and a quick exodus to the loo followed, leaving Tadhg and Pete alone for a moment.

"Did you know about the Cork ones coming here?" asked Tadhg.

"I had heard something about it Tadhg, they wanted to meet you."

"Fuck off!"

"No, straight up. Turns out you're a bit of a celebrity down in Baltimore."

"Me? What the fuck y'on about? Sure I've never even been there."

"You were born down there ye boy ye…in the pub! The only person with that honour. Ye lived there for a couple of years before moving up north," informed Pete.

"In the pub?"

"No, in Baltimore."

"But Ma never said anything about it."

"No I wouldn't blame her either. After the stable that's just about the maddest place to get born I ever heard of."

"What! What are you fuckin' talkin' about?" demanded Tadhg.

"Can you imagine the scene in the tavern? In the middle of a session too I heard," said Pete.

"Hardly her fault, I mean you just can't say right junior out ye come," replied Tadhg indignantly.

"I know. You're right. Don't shoot the messenger. They say you came out to a set of reels."

"You mean the fuckers kept playin'?"

"Aye well they didn't know what was wrong. It was mostly men and they just thought she had a sore stomach."

"A sore stomach! Fuckin' right it was a sore stomach," said Tadhg. "Jesus Christ. Spill!"

"Well according to Mick the Flick your Ma lay down under the table and started – you know – making them fuckin' women's noises. I think they did stop eventually but it was too late to move 'er.

"Don't tell me," said Tadhg, "they got hot water and towels?"

"Aye sort of," answered Pete. "It was more hot whisky and beer mats."

"Jesus fuckin' wept," said Tadhg, with a smile.

He couldn't help but see the funny side of it.

"And where's them Cork ones at now?"

"Aye well I had to call them there and explain ye'd fucked off up to Ballycastle. They're away on but they'll see us in Baltimore over the Fiddle Fair more than likely. I'll tell you more later," said Pete quickly.

The others were back and ready for the road.

22. In Nomine Patri et Fili

Pete quickly negotiated the busy roads around Madden's and was soon on the M1 heading south. Belfast, having recently undergone a major facelift in this area, was melting tidily into the distance behind them. Bank holiday afternoon drivers were taking their cars for a walk and the mood was chilled. They passed Hillsborough, Dromore then Banbridge and soon Tadhg noticed the signs for Newry.

Well well, the start of it all.

In Nomine Patri et Fili Missionary College was a just up the road and Tadhg was bursting to get a scoot around it but he could think of no excuse that would work.

Fuck sake, these ones wouldn't go to mass in a blue fit, never mind visit a missionary college.

Once again however, fate would lean in and tap his shoulder.

In Nomine Patri et Fili College Fair
A Day for all the Family
Bank Holiday Monday
from 12pm

There it was as big as life and written in black and white.

"Did you see that sign?" said Ogee.

"I did," answered Tadhg along with a few 'ayes' from the others.

"You know those things are generally good craic. There's always an oul' band playin' you know, burgers and all…" offered McLynn.

"Drink?" asked O'Connell.

"Fuck aye, beer tents usually," answered Ogee.

"Eh Pete…what say you to a small detour? You know just for one?" asked O'Malaigh.

Pete didn't answer and instead put his foot on the accelerator.

"Ach big man," said O'Malaigh, "I suppose that means no?"

"No it means we'll be there quicker," he answered looking over at Tadhg.

"Sweet," said Ogee, "sweet to the beat."

After a few moments Pete took the turn that led into In Nomine Patriet Fili College and immediately Tadhg heard the priest's words. His parents' secret affair began on this spot many years before and now here he was retracing their steps. Down the tree lined driveway they went.

"Here it's like something out of Dallas," said O'Malaigh, showing his age.

Although it was quite early still, just approaching two, there were quite a few about. Families were just dandering at their leisure, kids evading parents' wishes and fathers, who'd rather be pulling pints, pushing prams.

"Right lads," said Pete, "I'm goin' in to see one of the missionaries, he's an oul family friend. So…say…meet ye back here at half three?"

"That sounds dead on our fella," said Ogee.

The six got out of the car and Pete set off the few hundred yards to the grand building which served to house the missionaries and cater for functions, religious retreats and all manner of bible thump.

Tadhg watched him go as the five headed straight to the beer tent. They were the first there. Inside there were about twenty wooden tables with long benched seats attached lined up in two rows of ten. McLynn hit the bar and got the drinks in.

"The big lad seems a decent enough skin," said Ogee.

"Aye, so far so good. I mean we only met him last night," said O'Malaigh.

Tadhg wasn't altogether convinced. Who was he away to see?

23. In God We Fuss

Fr Dower was in a bit of a state. As well as sitting up half the night writing to his dead former girlfriend his bowels were now well and truly irritated. He had pains in his stomach and he though his backside was going to cave in.

"I know Lord, I probably deserve all I get but c'mon this is a bit much," he prayed.

He delivered a rather abstract early mass and those dedicated few that showed up were a little concerned at his demeanour. His sermon was only three minutes long and barely scratched the surface of St Paul's endless epistles to the Corinthians.

"Are you alright Father?" asked Mrs McIntyre.

She prided herself on early mass attendance. She was firmly set on the last lap of her life but not the worst by any means. She just liked to know what was going on.

"Ah yes of course, Annie," replied Fr Dower.

"It's just that mass yesterday and today was a little…well…short."

"Oh, was it? I didn't think so Annie. There's many's a one would probably say it was too long," he replied with a smile, hoping to deflect her interrogation with charm.

She wasn't having it.

"Well father these days you know you have a devoted if small congregation and I for one enjoy your opinions on the bible. You know my grandchildren don't go at all. No matter what I say and I wonder is God punishing me through them?"

Christ, this is all I need.

"Ah now Annie, God is love. He wouldn't punish someone as devoted as you. He could be doing with a few more like you I'd suggest."

On with the charm offensive.

"Maybe you're right Father…"

Thank God, now I can get my head straight.

"…but you know…,"

Shit.

"Yes Annie…"

"You know we are born sinners," she continued, "…and the road to Heaven is long with many bends…"

Wish I'd thought of that one.

"….He works in mysterious ways…"

No shit.

"Indeed, indeed…hmmm," he priested.

Time for some of the moves he'd picked up in In Nomine Patri et Fili.

"Sure we can only do our best Annie and if we fall short we have to rely on good people like you to help us along," he answered, taking her hand and giving it a squeeze.

Annie headed off like a child in a sweet shop. To get some priest time was a joy. Fr Dower walked slowly back past the shop and the car park. In the distance he could see the local hurling pitch.

I wish there was a game on.

He rubbed his gurgling tummy.

"Father."

It was Annie.

Christ the night.

"Ah Annie, you're back," he smiled.

"Yes father I was just wondering who that young lad was at your door yesterday morning?"

Fr Dower's bowels flipped and did a back somersault. She must have seen him on her way to mass. He thought he would lose his breakfast right there over the top of her lovely cream coloured mass coat.

"Em…ah…now…ah yes…that was…oh dear me Annie…look at that," he said in a sweat, staring over her shoulder.

Her eyes didn't leave his face.

"The young fellow…yes… a tourist. German. Lost you know. On a bike ride round the coast. They do call by from time to time, he was looking for directions."

He wondered would she buy it.

"You sent him on the right path I'm sure."

"Indeed, Annie," he smiled.

Away she went again, her curiosity sated for now.

If she only knew the half of it.

He walked slowly back to the house, down through the leafy lane and through the white painted steel gates. He gazed at the remains of the chrysanthemums.

To Hell with this. Baltimore it is.

He would explain to God later.

24. Dancers

"Fuckin' hell, that would do your heart good," exclaimed O'Malaigh as he set the pints down on the table.

"What's that?" asked Tadhg.

"Yer one. There look, behind you."

All eyes fell upon a very attractive young woman with short mouse brown hair entering the beer tent.

"Christ what ye wouldn't do to that," drooled McLynn.

"She'd ate ye for breakfast," laughed O'Malaigh.

She was wearing jeans and a black t-shirt with a logo emblazoned across it in white.

"It's the four dancin' alcoholics of the apocalypse…and a fine stage they have too," smiled Ogee.

"The wha'?" asked McLynn.

"The Ballyshannon Folk Festival t-shirt you tube. I do believe the ice will be easy enough broken," said O'Malaigh and headed off in her direction, pint in hand.

"Hornball," said Ogee.

"Fuck," said Tadhg, "she's a cracker."

She walked to the side of the tent where there was a space between the benches. There were five foldaway chairs on the ground and she began to flip them open and set them out in a crescent shape. A dead give-away for some sort of musical gathering. O'Malaigh was within striking distance.

"What about ye?" he began, standard first line.

She set the last of the chairs and turned around. It seems good looking girls have an inbuilt ejit avoidance device. Whatever her name was walked straight past O'Malaigh to the bar. Once there she ordered a pint of Guinness.

"Jesus, she drinks Guinness," said Tadhg dreamily.

O'Malaigh looked over at his audience, his face had 'challenge to be met' written all over it. He was not to be outdone by this first repost.

It seems some blokes, good looking or otherwise, have an inbuilt 'anti ejit avoidance device' which is triggered invariably by the triggering of the girl's 'ejit avoidance' technology. O'Malaigh's equipment appeared in fine working order.

He walked up beside her at the bar.

"I see you've been to Ballyshannon," he began.

"You don't miss a thing," she replied coolly.

"Hard to miss," he laughed, looking.

"I have eyes mate. You might want to look in them first."

"Oh I mean em..."

O'Malaigh let his eyes linger. He had to think fast otherwise the game was up.

"Sorry, 'tis genetic. Force of habit."

"Like wankin'."

Touché.

"What year were you there?" he asked, in a 'can we start again tone'.

"Every year. Why do you ask?" she replied, not a bit impressed.

"Well you'll have seen me playin' there then," he said.

"You? Oh aye?" she replied dismissively.

"Aye we did indeed, me and the lads at the table there. It was in '98 at the Gig Rig in the Diamond. A couple of afternoon slots we had."

"1998...," she said trying to recall that particular year, which is very difficult. Fleadhs and festivals have a habit of merging into one long hazy weekend in the memory bank.

"Well now you come to mention it, you have a familiar looking face. What do you play?" she asked.

"Ah now, I could tell but I'd probably have to kill ye," laughed O'Malaigh.

"No, I can't believe he came out with that fuckin' line," giggled Ogee.

Tit, thought McLynn.

"Kill me? Jesus you can keep it," she answered, not getting the joke.

Well, of course she got the joke. She just didn't find it funny and was going to make him squirm a bit.

"Ach well I'll probably only have to break your back," fired in O'Malaigh in an attempt to rekindle her interest.

A slight smile. "What did ye call yourselves?" she asked.

"Tradition," replied O'Malaigh.

"Interesting name," she answered, not altogether impressed.

"Aye well names are hard enough to think up," he answered.

"Obviously," she quipped, smiling. "Tradition eh? Well now you mention it I think I saw your name in the programme right enough. Well fair play to yiz. Ye must be decent enough to have played there."

"Ah now, we're alright," said O'Malaigh modestly. "Sure come over and say hello. What's your name by the way?"

"I could tell you but I'd have to cut your balls off!" she replied, winked and walked ahead to the table. From behind he noticed something in her bag, the unmistakeable rectangular outline of a flute box.

Result.

25. Just in case

Fr Dower looked once more into his garden, in some ways he felt it summed up his present state of mind…well manicured, pleasant, but with a bloody great clump of wreckage in the middle. His stomach was beginning to grumble too.

"Oh nice one, Lord," he moaned and reached into his pocket for a Bisodol. The little white tablets helped ease his inner pains and though most people took Rennies he was a Bisodol devotee.

It was Monday and he had arranged to take off on Wednesday with the bishop but what with all the excitement he didn't think he could wait.

"How the Hell am I gonna work this?" he asked himself.

His clocks ticked and he stared into their faces, hoping for inspiration. He was quickly leaving behind any calmness and his thoughts now began to cascade down through his brain hitting the stones of uncertainty below.

"I'll get sacked…defrocked even or de-collared…or whatever it is they do," he said aloud. The walls made good listeners.

He looked at the phone atop the little wooden table with its feminine curved legs and round platform. It was an old fashioned phone where you put your finger in and spun it round at the appropriate number. Its ring sounded like the number thirty three bus but Fr Dower didn't mind. Its appearance would not make the call to the bishop any easier.

He picked the beige receiver and opened the phone book.

"Bishop O'Hara, oh…two…eight….five…eight…ummm…uh huh…two," he mumbled.

The ringing tone began.

Oh Christ!

"Hello…" came a voice.

"Hel -…"

"You are through to Bishop O'Hara's residence; he is not available to…"

Bloody answering machine.

"…take your call, please leave a message."

The vernacular had got the better of him again and no mistake but such were his nerves he hardly noticed.

"Ah yes, Bishop O'Hara…Fr Eugene Dower here in Ballycarry parish…I need a…a…few days off. Sooner than I thought…yes…urgent family business. Please call me back…thank you…God bless…bye."

Fr Dower put the phone receiver gently back into its cradle.

Great!

He headed upstairs a little frustrated. He had built up a head of steam to make that call only for it to be nulled by the unsatisfactory halfway house of leaving a message. Now he would have to wait on a return call. His stomach gave a low gurgle and he quickly downed another Bisodol. He decided he would pack a few clothes as he waited. He did not have much to worry about here as the priest's wardrobe held few surprises. He had ordinary clothes somewhere.

"Black shirt…black trousers," he mumbled. "Says it all really…"

He flicked his hand amongst the hangers and threw the shirts on the bed. He reached up to the top of the wardrobe and pulled down his suitcase.

God, I've hardly used this since Dublin.

The case was one of those old small hard bodied brown types. In fact Fr Dower thought he must have grown enormously since as it didn't seem big enough to hold more than a pair of shoe laces. However, unlike today's veritable sleeping bag size cases this was deep and as he placed his clothes inside he was happy he still had it. The two old spring loaded latches were carefully thumb pushed down until he heard them click shut.

He allowed himself a smile.

"Dublin indeed," he said.

Bollox!

The phone was ringing.

26. The Temptations

"You wouldn't have a few friends would you?" asked Tadhg as the girl sat down at the table.

"Here lads I'd tell you her name but…well, she wouldn't tell me?" said O'Malaigh, feigning hurt.

"Of course I have friends," she answered looking at Tadhg seriously.

"Only askin' love," he said quickly, a little thrown by her cold stare.

He was quickly warmed by her ensuing smile and she offered her hand.

"Roisín," she said. "Rosie. We're playing a few tunes here in a while."

"Tadhg," he answered, and shook her hand.

"What's the craic?"she asked.

She gave a good stout handshake and Tadhg's heart skipped a beat.

How did he get her fuckin' name? mused O'Malaigh.

"Well Rosie, if I told ya we were all heading for West Cork on a spur of the moment whim with a gorilla for a driver and nowhere to stay would that shed any light?" replied Tadhg.

"Fiddle Fair perchance?"

"Good lookin' and clever!" exclaimed O'Malaigh before he could help himself.

He quickly hid his face in a gulp of Guinness fearing that he'd blown whatever cool he thought he might have left.

"You said it," agreed O'Connell, helping his mate.

"Ah now lads," said Rosie, "I bet ye say that to all the girls."

"Those that'd look at them," snapped McLynn with a grin, not wanting to miss out. This lassie was up for a bit of banter and that was good enough for him.

"So ye play the flute I see?" said O'Malaigh, not wishing to lose the initiative. After all, he had done the ground work.

"I do indeed," she replied.

"What sort of flute do you have? A Sam? Or a Grinter maybe?" he asked, happy to show off his knowledge on the best flute makers.

"It's a Sam actually," replied Rosie. "Do you play yourself?"

"Ach I used to you know but the fags have me lungs bucked. Still love listening to it though. Mostly whistle these days."

"Good man, but you don't still smoke do ye?" she asked.

"Well I do but I usually only borrow them after a few drinks. You know how it is?"

"Borrow? Ha. Never bothered with them. Not the ordinary ones anyway. Have smoked the odd roley, but try not to these days, fucks up the breathin' altogether."

Well if she didn't have enough going for her already doesn't she go and start swearing like a football fan.

Class! thought Tadhg.

Ride! thought O'Malaigh.

"So ye're heading down to Cork eh? How ye travellin'?" asked Tadhg, her sweet cursing voice resounding in his ears.

"Well of course I'd be asking you lads for a lift…" she began.

O'Malaigh nearly choked on a slug of Stout.

"…but there's a few of us travelling down in a wee while."

"Oh aye," chirped in Ogee, "your sisters?"

"Ha, no not exactly, more like sisters in arms if ye know what I mean?"

Orgy! thought McLynn.

He quickly looked around to make sure he hadn't said it out loud.

"Aye they'll be here in a minute. I think they're out looking at one of the clothes stalls, you know like women do," she laughed.

They can do what they like, thought O'Malaigh. *If they look like you this could be some party.*

As Rosie lifted her glass they all heard a load yoo-hoo from behind and in they came. They five lads turned to see four fine looking lassies dip in under the flaps of the beer tent. In a moment they had spotted Rosie and were heading over to join her.

"These'll be the friends then?" offered Tadhg.

"You're not a bit slow Sherlock," grinned Rosie in reply.

Well if the four girls didn't just dander up as cool as you like and sit down. The lads sat back and enjoyed the view. Each of the girls carried a musical instrument too and left them down at their feet.

"Right," said the blond haired one, "who's buyin'?"

The lads were landed. Women that drank, cursed and played trad. After a moment they began to make as if they were going to get their purses.

"What'll ye have?" smiled Ogee, bridging that chivalrous gap.

A quick order of pints and bottles of various beers was made along with one fizzy water.

"So you got the short straw then?" Tadhg asked a long haired red head. "You either don't drink or you're drivin' eh?

"Aye, I'm driving today. But not tomorrow," she winked back.

The introductions then took place and soon the lads had met Eileen, Sarah, Cassie and Sorcha. In a few moments the early banter was in full flow as each sussed out who and how they might attract. The initial skirmishes had gone well as they found out a little about each other. The girls were all from the Newry area, Mayobridge, Rostrevor and Burren and played sessions together. It was going well and would've continued had the Pockel not intervened. He barrelled into the tent spilling bibles onto the grass.

"Right you pricks, come on to fuck. We gotta run…the cops are comin'!"

27. High Tailing

"Wha?" gasped Tadhg.

"I'm fuckin' serious. Look, just get in the car and I'll tell ye the craic, c'mon," gasped Pete. The tone of his voice did not disguise any mirth at all; there was no punch line on the way.

"Aw fuck me. Typical," sighed Ogee. He could see a bit of tongue wrestling with the girls quickly disappear before him.

"What did ye do?" he asked as they gathered up their instruments.

"Are ye away?" asked Rosie, "without even a goodbye?"

"Looks like it," replied Tadhg, "will we see you in Baltimore?"

"Ye will," she replied.

"Sorry girls but I gotta get these halyins outta here. Don't let on ye seen us," shouted the Pockel on his way back to the car.

In the distance the wail of sirens could be heard.

"Hurry to fuck up," yelled Pete.

The lads gathered all and necked what remained in their glasses. In a few moments they had piled in to the car once more. Pete started her up and spun the wheels on the grass as it struggled for grip.

"C'mon ye fucker," Pete roared.

Suddenly the car took off and was skimming down the long lane out of In Nomine Patri et Fili at a considerable rate.

"What the fuck?" asked Tadhg, flicking through the thin crisp pages of one the many New Testaments Pete flung onto the seats.

"I think I killed one of them oul' priests," said Pete a bit sheepishly.

"Ha!" laughed O'Malaigh, a man with very little sympathy for men and women of the cloth.

"What did you do that for?" asked McLynn.

By now they had reached the main road and took the right turn toward Newry.

"Pure fluke. I was only lookin' around. I did a retreat there once with school. Third year I think. One of them said to call back anytime," replied Pete, now in a bit more control of himself and the car.

"Retreat? Christ, you're not a fuckin' Jesus freak are ye?" asked O'Malaigh.

"No way but that was the last time I was here. Must be 20 odd years ago. Anyway I got chattin' to one of them oul' boys."

"Talking about what exactly?" asked Tadhg.

"It wasn't about The Last Supper anyway," shouted O'Connell from the back.

"Ah no, just this and that and me being there once, ye know. Well didn't he go and tell me to 'take a handful of bibles for your friends'. I was gonna tell him no but sure I took a handful to keep him happy and then I sat on him."

"You did what?"demanded Tadhg.

"Ach he was that wee you'd hardly see him and he sat in the chair just behind me when I was gathering up them bloody bibles. His leg was out, I hit it, lost my balance and sat on him. Fuck he didn't look good."

"Ha, no wonder, you plank," laughed O'Connell.

"Aye, well I got up as quick as I could but I swear I heard his legs crack. I turned round and he was near all sunk into the arse of the armchair. I says 'fuck this' and legged it. Yer wee doll behind the counter must a thought I'd killed him."

The dual carriage into Newry now thinned itself into one lane and they noticed an ambulance whiz past with the sirens ablaze.

"That'll be for your handiwork no doubt," said Tadhg.

"Time we got across the border," replied Pete.

Pete headed for the bypass thus avoiding the web that is Newry centre traffic.

"In Newry Town I was bred and born..." sang O'Malaigh, pulling the first line from that grand old song out of his memory bank.

In a few moments they were on the hill out of Newry and the North. To their left the kingdom of Mourne stretched wide and distant and their right revealed the majesty of the hills of South Armagh.

"We're in God's own country now," said Tadhg proudly.

"He must've had a lot of countries," quipped back Ogee.

"Ah yer balls. Ye Belfasties wouldn't know a mountain if it came up and give yiz a blow job," snapped back Tadhg.

"I'd climb that mountain," sighed O'Malaigh.

Pete was showing no mercy to the car and they were past the old border check point in no time.

"We're in Ireland now boys," said Pete, with a grin. "Breathe in that free air."

"'Tis the same air all over ye twat. What happened?" snapped Tadhg.

"Ach Tadhg ye have to admit there's nothing like crossing that feckin' border," said O'Malaigh.

"Well lads," began Tadhg, "can you touch the border? No? Do you see it? Smell the bloody thing? Well then fuck it, this is Ireland top to bottom and to hell with all that other shite."

"Aye right enough," said Ogee, "no point talking politics without a few pints. It's a pain in the arse anyway. C'mon Pete give her the welly."

Pete pressed on and the white lines on the road blended into one beneath them.

28. Phone Call

Oh Jesus, Mary and St Joseph, thought Fr Dower.

Five rings…six…seven…

Answer it you leper!

"Hello, Fr Dower speaking how may I help?" he said in his best phone voice.

"Ah Eugene is that yourself? 'Tis Eamon here, I got your message. Is everything ok?" asked the bishop.

"Eamon thanks for calling back so soon, you're keeping well I trust?"

Got to stall him for a moment. How am I going to put this?

"Yes fine, thank God. In fact I was thinking of coming up to the glens soon and was going to call with you, on the QT of course. So you need a few days off? It seems quite sudden. Are you sure all is well?"

I should just tell him the bloody truth, he thought, then,

Don't be a fool. That would be the end of you.

"Ah yes, well, you see I got a call from out of the blue yesterday evening. You remember my aunt Geraldine? She's the last on my mother's side…"

"I seem to recall you mentioning her once or twice…"

"Well it turns out that she's been taken into Daisy Hill hospital. They rang me as her next of kin and it looks like the end."

"Ah Eugene I'm sorry to hear that indeed. Is there anything I can do?"

"Well not really Eamon, it's just that I'll have to scoot off down to Newry ASAP and well I don't have cover."

What a tangled web…sure all he has to do is ring the bloody hospital…

"Yes that is a problem. However, in such circumstances we must rally round. Leave it with me I'll see who's available. I'm sure they can help. Pass on my best to your aunt. I'll call you shortly, good bye."

Oh my good Jesus, I didn't think I'd be such a good liar but I suppose it's not surprising is it?

"Ok goodbye and thank you," he answered and put down the phone.

I wonder who'll come out. Probably Fr Monotonous! Contrary oul' shite. Sour oul' head on him too. The parish'll never forgive me.

He wasn't bothered who came out. The parishioners would survive without him for a bit. He had Tadhg on his mind. He looked around the living room and heard the clocks. They would go on with their job no matter what. He looked at them one by one and listened. Their internal workings each dividing time ever so slightly differently, until every now and again they would be in unison and then as quickly tick their own ticks.

He smiled and left the room, closing the door gently behind him. His old case waited patiently at the door. From the table beneath the mirror in the hall he picked up his bible, its old leather binding felt smooth in his hand.

Well Lord I'm not sure what I'm doin' but perhaps ye might keep an eye on me?

He opened the door to see Annie staring at him, her hand just reaching for the knocker.

Jesus woman!

"Oh! You're going away, Father?"

29. Foot Down

"Here big man, ye can take yer foot off the pedal there," said Ogee. "No sign of the cops that I can see."

Pete's face was locked in concentration. His huge lower jaw jutted out under his hairy nose. He would've reminded anyone who knew of a young Bruce Forsyth in this pose hence perhaps his 'Bruce of the Forsythes' carry on in Tom's.

Without a word Pete looked quickly into the rear view mirror and headed out onto the wrong lane of the little piece of dual carriageway just before the well known local Carrickdale Hotel.

"Hi, what the fuck are y'at?" shouted Tadhg, suddenly feeling panic invade his half dozing head.

"Fuck sake Pete, what's the craic?" asked Ogee from behind.

All attention now on a not too distant 18-wheeled truck heading their way. "Ach dry your fuckin' eyes," came the terse reply.

Pete buried the right foot again and the car lunged forward. The finer details of the lorry's front grill and number plate to name but two of the many things that make up a lorry front were burning themselves into Tadhg's consciousness. He had come a long way and wasn't about to end it here at the whim of Pete's impression of Michael Schumacher. But that was just it, he couldn't speak or even scream or had the moment arisen, shit himself.

Pete bombed on closer and closer now. The lorry was about fifty feet from the start of the lane they were on. If it joined them on this lane that would be that. The engine in the people carrier squealed in complaint and the lads stopped breathing. The glaring lights of the lorry, all of them, the top ones, bottom ones, middle ones all began to flash and Tadhg became aware of the singular rasp of the lorry's horn, the one that kids ask for with a pulling down motion.

"Aw fuck it anyway," said Tadhg.

But it wasn't the end. Whatever Pete was at he just managed to get onto the single lane at the end of the dual carriageway about two seconds before the beast of a lorry roared past.

"That was close," smiled Pete to his transfixed audience.

He expected applause.

"I've been meanin' to try that for years. Newry thing, ye know."

The faces were locked in dread and were now changing subtly to anger.

"And you chose now? Jesus Christ!" yelled O'Malaigh.

"Whaddya mean?" protested Pete. "Sure it was only a bit a craic."

"Craic?"gasped Ogee. "Craic? Here, stall the wagon."

Pete pulled into the side of the road not a good puck out from the door of The Carrickdale Hotel. This was the spot for weddings and functions for miles around and looked like someone had lifted it out of Monaco or somewhere like that and planted it along the main Dublin road. It was spectacular.

"I need a fuckin' swally."

Ogee's tone was such that no one doubted just how angry he was.

"Right you looper, park 'er over there. We'll be in the bar," said Tadhg.

He got out with the rest and slammed the door shut. Pete moved the car slowly away over to the car park.

"Fuck me Tadhg, thon big tube near got us kilt," said O'Connell.

"Aye I know but ye know what? I don't think it took a fidge out of him."

The fact that he was still alive and the adrenalin cascade were now beginning to mix.

"The big fuckin' ejit did that for a laugh?" wheezed a breathless McLynn, only now regaining the sight in his eyes.

The five dandered in on shaky legs to the wide expanse of the Carrickdale front bar.

"Ah balls. Any of yous got Euros?" asked O'Malaigh with one eye on a ten year old Scottish malt he was fond of.

"Ah balls, use the queen. She's gotta be good for something," said O'Connell.

"I'll lose a fortune...fuckin' Mexican money," snapped back O'Malaigh.

The need for slurp outweighed the financial sting of the exchange rate. In a moment the five had their bevies and were wondering how they would survive the remainder of the journey.

30. Out the Gap

"Annie!"

Excrement!

"Going away? Em...yes. Yes, family bother you know, very sad. Last minute type of thing," answered Fr Dower not really looking at the busy little woman.

He knew if he did catch her eye for more than a millisecond he would be getting the third degree.

"Family bother? Nothing serious I hope? It's just that there's an important meeting tonight regarding the contents of this week's bulletin and you really should be there, Father," she answered, following his every move.

Fr Dower placed his suitcase in the back seat so that as Annie spoke his backside was all she could see. He stayed bent over for an extra moment and seriously contemplated breaking wind but slowly turned to face her.

"Oh Annie, I'm so sorry but I completely forgot about that. It has been a very hectic morning what with one thing and another."

He could see the chrysanthemum carnage over her shoulder.

"So what should we do, Father? The bulletin is as close to God's word as a lay person can get. I really think we should steer the contents away from hurling results and add more scripture. For the good of the parish," she continued.

"You know Annie, I have thought long and hard about this and you have helped me enormously make up my mind."

"Glad I could help," replied Annie.

"Yes, it's that small minded, selfish and frankly baffling attitude you wear so well that has held up decisions on committees like ours for years. Tell them to write whatever they like and I insist on all hurling results, fixtures and injury updates being included!"

Annie was aghast and her lips pursed as if hooked on a line.

"But, Father..."

"But Annie...don't you see? It's a bulletin! Not the Gospel according to you. It's a link to explain what's going on in and around the parish. It is not a letter from St Paul to the bloody Corinthians!"

Wow, that felt good.

"If you'll excuse me Annie I have to go. We can discuss the outcomes further after the weekend."

He walked around to the driver's door and got in. Annie followed him around in a bit of a daze. For years she had been a confidante or at least that's what she thought. She enjoyed walking down to the car park with him after each service and making sure her neighbours saw them too. She wasn't about to be brushed off like an annoying insect.

"So do I take it that we include the Camogie results too?"

"Yes. In the name of God, yes! And while you're at it I want the price of hoggets and calves and barley straw in it too."

"Well I'm afraid I'll have to hold a meeting."

"You do that Annie," said Fr Dower.

With that he closed the door and slowly drove the car up through the large white gates that guarded the driveway. He could see Annie in the rear view mirror speaking into her mobile phone.

That oul' crone. I've probably not heard the end of this one.

But his thoughts were on the road ahead. At this particular moment he cared little for the likes of Annie and took the right turn toward Ballycastle once more.

God, I've been wanting to tell that oul' bag to wise up for years. But was I too rough on her? Whaddya think? Eh?

"Fucking silence as usual!" said Fr Dower out loud.

It's not that I doubt you Lord but you know a wee word every now again, anything would do, even a burp.

But there would be no Heavenly wind heading his way today. This day was his day. The dalliances of youth and their consequences had landed in a heap in his garden and he needed to go.

31. Curran

The five had blown the froth off a couple by the time Pete joined them.

"Here he is, fuckin' Sterling Moss," snapped Ogee, still angry at the almost harbinger of his doom.

"Ach wise up. Didn't ye live through the 'Troubles'? Panicking over a wee dander down the road. Catch yourself on," replied Pete, in no mood for apology.

"We're still here and we've a long way to go yet," said Tadhg diffusing the situation.

"No thanks to Buck fuckin' Rogers," said O'Malaigh. "Here, what time is it?"

"Twenty to three," answered O'Connell.

"Aye, thought so. Look 'tis still about six hours to Baltimore and I'm in no rush back into the car, no offence big man. Tadhg, you must know somewhere about here where you'd get a few tunes. I say we chill out a while, go and have a tune and get going first thing tomorrow afternoon."

"Afternoon?" said Pete.

"Aye well you know what I mean? Anything before nine in the mornin' is the middle of the night," said O'Connell. "Whaddya think Tadhg?"

"Sounds like a plan to me. I know a class wee spot in Dundalk, McManus's," answered Tadhg who didn't need too much persuading when it came to tunes.

"But this is Monday Tadhg. Not many sessions about on a Monday," said Ogee.

"Aye but we can always ask. If I know Curran he'll be up for tunes like a rat up a drain pipe."

Alphonsis Curran was well known in the Dundalk area. As well being a multi instrumentalist and singer his drinking exploits were the stuff of legend. Indeed his many battle scars had proved quite the aphrodisiac to impressionable young tourists and students, a fact that he took liberal advantage of.

"Christ aye. Curran. Jesus do ye mind him at the fleadh last year?" said O'Connell en route back from the bar.

"Aye sure wasn't I with him?" said Tadhg.

"What happened?" asked Pete.

"Ach he got fuckin' snottered drunk..."

"Surprise surprise," quipped Ogee.

"...and got arrested for indecent assault."

"What?"

"Aye an' him tryin' to be the good Samaritan an' all. Ye see this wee lassie had had far too much Aftershock or WKD or whatever them wains drink and collapsed in the street. Her friends wanted to get her home. So, upon the scene danders Dr Octopus and goes to pick her up. Well he comes round behind her, gets her sittin' up and puts his hands under her oxsters.

"Fair play to him," said Pete.

"Fair play my hole. His hands didn't stop at her oxsters. Says he 'fuckin' jug alert' and cops a feel of yer ones baps in front of everybody."

"Who dares wins eh?" laughed McLynn.

"Dirty bastard," chuckled O'Malaigh.

"Aye that was alright 'til the fuckin' guards came along. I doubt if yer wee one would've even remembered but this woman guard comes up and stops him with a slap on the back of the head."

"Oh and then they arrested him?" asked Pete.

"No, if only. Turned out the woman guard was Polish and had perfect English of course but no Irish."

"So?"

"So... she gives out about leaving the wee one alone and tells him not to be fondling collapsed wee girl's breasts in the street."

"Job done?"

"Not at all. Curran's an old school Gael, fluent in the oul mother tongue and doesn't do English sports. Says he, 'I demand to be cautioned in Irish. Would someone please arrest me in my own language?'

"And what happened?"

"Well after they eventually got his hands welded off yer one he fuckin' reared up and stated singing Dúlaman, an oul' Gaelic song of course.

After a bit, two big Cavan guards dumped him into the back of the squad car in old fashioned Garda language. I went with him just to keep him right. He calmed down anyway, got a caution and was told to wise up. Just got carried away with himself."

"Christ...and this is the guy we're meeting?"

"Ach he's grand you know, big softy really. Just loves women ...and drink...and tunes."

"He'll fit right in then," said Pete.

32. El Paso

The drink had had the desired effect. The lads had relaxed sufficiently from their near death experience to contemplate getting back into the car with Pete. Pete himself was keen to get on.

"Here, lads it's time we were outta here. I don't mind stopping in McManus's but we need to get a room or somethin' sorted for tonight. I am not sleepin' in the car with you smelly bastards."

"Ha! Listen to him," replied Ogee.

"Fair enough Pete," said Tadhg. "C'mon."

With that the five finished off their glasses and headed outside. The day had moved on and the first whisperings of evening could be heard on the wind.

"Here, I'm fuckin' starvin'," said Ogee. "Belly thinks my throat's cut."

"Aye, good idea. We'll get up to Dundalk and get a Chinese or something," said O'Malaigh. The others agreed and the plan had been made as if by magic. Chinese, pints, tunes, pints, songs...pints.

"Sounds good to me," said O'Connell, "but what about somewhere to stay?"

"Ach would you ever wise up, sure there's rooms upstairs in McManus's. Ye get a good rate if ye play a few tunes. I sort of know one of the local musos there, friend of Curran's. We had tunes at the fleadh a few times. He'll sort us out," said Tadhg, buoyed up again with the few pints and bursting for a few more.

"Dead on," said O'Connell.

"And what about forty fingers or whatever ye call him? Does he not have a house?" asked Pete.

"Curran? Fuck me ye wouldn't sleep in his place. He still lives with his Ma," laughed Tadhg.

"Jesus!" said Pete, "and I thought I was the last one."

"What? Do you live with yer ma too?" asked McLynn.

"Fuckin' sures. Sure why wouldn't I? Fuckin' home made grub, shirts and all washed and ironed. Are ye mad? 'Tis great."

Lazy big shite, thought O'Malaigh.

"I have thon place in Ballycastle but that's just a wee holiday home really. Ma's great God love 'er. Eighty next birthday."

They re-entered Pete's car and he drove on up the road on the appropriate side. Tadhg had begun to think of his own mother as the conversation moved back and forth with the pros and cons of still living at home.

I should've stayed at home for a while longer. But then why would I have? Mum had her own stuff to get on with.

In the distance Dundalk came into view. That is to say signs for the world's worst bypass came into view. The Isle of Man sized roundabout was home to several large diggers and other road making wagons. They had been there for ages and the road was still nowhere near done.

"Left here Pete," said Tadhg.

"I'm not fuckin' blind ye ball bag," snapped back the driver.

"Alright big man, I was only keepin' ye right. This is the longest and worst excuse for a bypass in Ireland. In fact 'tis more like the Bermuda Triangle but you fire on and I'll let you know where to turn," replied Tadhg, aware that perhaps Pete was a bit tender about his driving after the lorry critique.

Unfortunately for Tadhg he hadn't experienced the open air rabbit warren that is inner Dundalk for ages. Up and down and back and round and left and right they went.

"Ah for fuck sake!" snapped Ogee. "Do you have a notion where ye're goin'?"

"Hang on, hang on," replied Tadhg. "Ask yer man there."

Approaching them, walking a small terrier type dog came a middle aged gentleman. He was smartly dressed and had on him a three quarter length fawn coloured coat. Pete stopped the car and wound down the window.

"Here, our fella, would you know where a bar called McManus's is? This ejit here is givin' us directions this half hour and we're well lost."

As is the way the man briefly wore a quizzed look on his face. Perhaps the site of this man mountain with the squeaky Belfast voice brought the frown to his brow or perhaps it was his collection of dubious looking passengers. Whatever the cause, he snapped a quick 'Lie down' at the dog and replied.

"McManus's? De bar? I know it well. What de hell way did ye come in at all?"

"Third left off the bypass according to fuckin' twat-nav here," replied Pete looking scornfully at Tadhg.

"Ah Jaysus lad, sure that road's closed dis ten years..."

"What the fuck did he say?" whispered Ogee.

He was not at all used to the long round vowels of the Dundalk accent.

"Aye now... houl' on. Yes...aye...if you turn right at don lamp deyre and den first left. Ye can't miss it. Big house on de corriner," he concluded.

"Ah good man, cheers," replied Pete.

The man pulled a tug on the lead and proceeded on his way into the early evening. "Told ye," said Tadhg.

"Yer hole!"

Within a few minutes the narrow tree lined streets yielded up the Promised Land. There it was, all lit up on the corner as foretold... McManus's.

33. Few Tunes

"Here this is a bit fuckin' tight," puffed Pete as he struggled to get his frame through the wee double doors.

"Is this the fuckin' leprechauns' entrance? Christ!"

He had similar feelings at Tom's doors in Ballycastle.

"Our fella," said Ogee, "time ye got the tracksuit on and got off your arse. Get up to the bar and get a round in."

Pete quickly shouted a round. In most circumstances anyone who used that tone with Pete got a mouthful of his oversized knuckles. Pete and the lads squeezed into the little side bar. It really wasn't much bigger than a shoe box.

Like Madden's before, it had a breathable history and picture ornate walls. The bar stretched along the left hand side with coat hooks on one side. It was apparent that there was a lot more to this tavern as it disappeared beyond a wooden partition.

"Fuck! 'Iontach'! Jesus what would ye not do to yer one?" lusted McLynn on seeing the picture of one of the female members of that band.

"Her tits are talkin' to me," gurgled O'Connell.

"Aye, an' they're sayin' no fuckin' chance dick head," fired in Ogee, laughing.

"She worked here, sure," came a voice.

"Fuck, if I'd a known that," replied McLynn. "How do you know 'er?"

"I'm playin' here dis twenty years and many's the pint she gave me."

The bearer of this information sat tucked into the corner of the snug. He was a short and stocky framed man with a shock of curly brown hair.

"Ha, Aidan? What about ye? Haven't seen ye since thon night at the All Ireland. I'm not right yet! Is that all she gave ye?" asked Tadhg, not immune to her charms.

They shook hands warmly. The handshake of session veterans.

"What do you play?" asked McLynn.

"Fiddle and banjo."

"Powerful head for tunes this lad," said Tadhg, as introduction to the others. "You'll know Curran then?"

"Too well! Yes, he rang me there and said there'd be a few tunes."

"Great stuff, do ye mind if we join ye?" asked Ogee.

"Jesus, not at all. Sure Curran's sick lookin' at me. I knew there'd be a few about by the chat of him. I'm thinkin' ye are dem?"

"Indeed, that's us. All the way from Ballycastle via a wee stop here and there. What's yer name again mate?" asked O'Malaigh.

"Aidan Ó Conghaile."

"What did he say?" asked Ogee.

"That's Irish ye tit!" snapped back O'Malaigh. "The mother tongue."

"She's not my fuckin' Ma," retorted O'Connell, obviously not impressed with the sudden non English direction of the conversation.

"Whaddya mean 'not yer ma'?" asked O'Malaigh. "Ye want to learn a bit of your own language ye dose."

"Balls! Irish is as dead as thon fuckin' pint," replied O'Connell, looking over at a long abandoned half pint of lager.

"Here, fuck me lads," said Ogee, "we're here for a few tunes, no words in any language required."

The potentially awkward situation was immediately diffused. The Irish language debate was now a popular one over a few beers amongst musicians and the like. It often ended up as a history lesson in English brutality over eight hundred years and while the grievance was true Ogee didn't want anything to 'wreck his buzz'.

"O'Conghaile? Is that like... O'Connell?" asked O'Connell.

"It's the Gaelic version," replied Aidan.

"Christ, are we related? We could be!"

"Ha, I doubt it but ye never know," said Aidan smiling.

"Here get in there to fuck," said McLynn.

They moved seamlessly from the bar and got themselves into the large round table alongside Aidan. There were also two small round tables on full alert.

"Here, is there any seats...you know for locals? Don't want to be standing on anyone's toes like" asked O'Connell.

"No you're grand, sit down."

"Dead on, cheers."

Entrance granted.

The door opened again.

Curran!

"Cunts! Who's buying the drink?" he bellowed.

"Mind yer fuckin' language," snapped the bar man.

"Curran, ye big fucker. How the hell are ye?"asked Tadhg.

"I'll be better in about three minutes. Guinness there please Pádraig."

The barman headed off and began the poetic ritual that is a pint of good Guinness. Pete felt a pang on hearing the hiss of stout flood the glass.

"Here, big lad...ye gonna keep your knickers on the night?" asked O'Connell.

Pete got the message and he would just have the three.

"Ha fuckin' ha!" he snapped.

"So what brings ye all down here? Well Aidan," asked Curran, indulging in the habit of firstly asking a question and then acknowledging anyone he hadn't already said hello to in the one sentence. The rest of the lads started to release their instruments.

"Long story," answered Tadhg. "Sure we're here now. You still fit to sing a song or two?"

"There ye go," said the bar man suddenly appearing with the Guinness which he carefully steered over Curran's left ear and placed before him on the table.

"Ah Jesus, good man Pádraig. I've a mouth on me like Gandhi's flip flop."

"Aye so has yer Ma," snapped Aidan with a broad grin.

Curran almost ate the pint. He was half way down before coming up for breath.

"Ah fuck!" came his satisfied pant and he replaced the white streaked glass on the table.

The boys had found places for the instrument cases wherever they could. Indeed it's at such moments that guitar players and the like often wish they had learned the whistle. Still, after a few moments moving and pushing and lifting and cursing, the cases where stacked up in the small space behind the seat and the window so that they sat like an oddly headed audience.

Curran had caught the others up in that one gulp so much so that eyes now began to survey the remaining quantities in the glasses. Who would bite first? The musicians feigned interest, turning tuning pegs and putting their ears down to the strings or pushing in the connection at the top of the flute. No one wanted to get lumbered with the next round. Not for any other reason than having to go to the bar which would mean getting up, climbing out, climbing back and all that stuff.

"I'll go," said Pete, perfectly positioned at the edge of the table closest to the bar.

"Same again?"

No answer in words was needed.

The instruments were ready. The little electronic tuners were placed on the tops of the guitar and bouzouki. Tadhg trusted his ears because like most fiddlers he wouldn't have been caught dead using such a device.

The whistle and flute were low maintenance when it came to tuning, as of course was the drum. Ogee hit a few taps.

"Ye in tune?" joked Tadhg.

Then silence. Well, sort of silence. The moment had come for someone to strike the first note of the first set of tunes. It didn't last long and indeed the casual observer may well have missed it but it was there none the less and those in that concentrated company all knew it.

O'Malaigh led them.

Reels!

"Good man," said Aidan and immediately followed in behind.

Then Ogee on drum, tipping away. Then Tadhg, and as he brought the bow over the strings he felt relaxed, safe and excited all at once.

Here we go again.

34. Prayers of the Faithful

Eugene Dower had rarely felt so free. He was well on the way down the road and took a quick sideways glance at Loughbrickland with its little Union Jacked island in the middle.

Bloody flags.

Onward now towards Newry town. In recent years the powers that be in a slow day at work had bestowed upon Newry the ridiculous title of city.

City? City my arse!

It would always be the 'town' to him. The road thinned and thickened, singled and doubled and greyed and greened in front of him. The steady hum of engine and wind competed with the chat show he had going on his radio. Then he saw it.

'In Nomine Patri et Fili' - next left.

Well, well. I should go in and say hello. Do no harm I suppose. Will just skim over the ill aunt story.

As with the boys a little while before the tree lined lane bade him a gentle welcome. There were still a good number of people milling about in the grounds enjoying what was left of the festivities. He had been down this lane many times for seminars and retreats and all manner of ecumenical duty. This was different though. This time he had a son on his mind.

Secrets.

He took the right turn that lead to the front door of the great house itself. It reminded him of a Stormont for priests, all arches and Our Fathers. There he noticed an unusual amount of police cars and an ambulance. The ambulance men were in the process of stretchering out a grey haired gentleman who looked one good sneeze away from the coffin.

Fr Hamill. I thought he died years ago.

Eugene was confused entirely. He did not expect his erstwhile home to give him such a greeting. He parked and headed over to the action.

"Can I help?" he asked.

"No, we're sorted thanks, Father," replied the medic.

Eugene climbed the steps of the majestic beige building and headed in. Down into the beautifully tiled reception area he went to see a police man taking a statement and one of the resident missionaries.

"So you saw a large man, with big hands."

"Big hairy hands. Huge behind."

"Big hairy hands? Huge behind?"

"Yes."

Pete? No, couldn't be?

"And he crushed Fr Hamill?"

"Yes. Well no, not crushed exactly. Sat on him. It was an accident of momentum. The big chap didn't see Fr Hamill."

"And could you say where he was from by his accent at all?"

"Oh yes, definitely Belfast or Newry. Or Warrenpoint...possibly Rostrevor. No doubt."

"Uh huh. And what was he wearing Father?" continued the policeman.

"A large denim jacket and jeans. And he had black hair," answered the priest.

"OK, Father. And where did he go after his assault on Fr Hamill."

"It wasn't assault young man," said the priest.

Dirty Harry eh? thought Fr Dower.

"Ok, the 'accident'. Where did he go?"

"Straight out the front door like a bat out of – "

"The bathroom? 'Tis just down there -"said the missionary suddenly, giving directions to an under pressure medic who signalled from behind the policeman.

"-just through that door there," he finished, pointing to a solid oak door just down the hall.

"And did he take anything?" asked the policeman, now a little exasperated as to why he had been summoned at all.

"Well, yes...and he was carrying some bibles."

"Bibles?"

"Yes. We have lots. Would you like one?"

"No father, you're grand. I'll do without."

"Of course. Well on seeing Fr Hamill go down, Linda on reception called the police and ambulance. I really don't think he meant any harm but she feared the worst and here you are nonetheless."

"Hmm, and this was about an hour ago?"

"Yes. He then ran out as fast as he could looking quite flummoxed and loaded himself into a car with four or five others."

Crap, thought Fr Dower.

"They headed up the lane at some speed and that was the last we saw of them. A large silver car I think."

"I'll need car details and number plate if possible. I need to speak to him."

Fr Dower had to act fast. Who knew what would come out if Pete and his now outlaw friends were caught?

"That bloody programme has a lot to answer for?" he said earnestly and walked over with outstretched arms to the missionary answering the questions.

"Sean," he said and proceeded to hug him.

"Eugene!" replied the missionary. "Goodness you have picked a right day to visit. How are you at all? What programme?"

"Fr Ted."

"What?"

"Good show that," offered the policeman not sure what to expect next.

"No respect left," said Fr Dower. "Coming in here like that. Probably drunk off his head, looking for valuables to sell on for drugs and the like I'm sure."

"'Tis an awful state of affairs right enough but let's be honest Eugene, Fr Ted didn't really cause that much bother," he looked at the ground. "It was those sick bastards, God forgive me. Attacking children and then covering up."

Fr Dower breathed deeply. The attention had been moved from Pete for the minute.

Didn't see that coming, thought the policeman.

The law man had never heard a priest curse before and had replaced his pen for the moment. It was a dark topic for the clergy and suddenly the big man's antics seemed very insignificant.

"I know Sean, done for the lot of us so they did. Worst of it all, I knew a few of them. Teaching if ye don't mind, let loose in those schools. Ye wonder could we have done more? We should have done something. Jesus knows we're paying for it now."

"Would you like to press charges Father," said the cop, who had run out patience.

"No, we'll be ok. God forgive him."

"OK then fathers. If he comes back let us know, thanks."

The police said their goodbyes and left. The ambulance took Fr Hamill away and the calmness on which In Nomine Patri et Fili breathes returned.

"Ah Eugene, there are days when you wonder does God have a plan at all."

"Aye, I know Sean but you know what? We'll stick it out...'tis too late to stop now anyway. We'll say a prayer."

35. Fire Starter

The initial tunes had been played and, as if a serpent from the basket, the spirit of this particular session in Dundalk had begun to move. Not that you could see it of course but it was there casting its spell on musician and listener alike. The first tunes served as a loosener of mind and fingers, almost like a boxer bobbing and weaving against his opponent, throwing out testing punches to gauge strength and prepare for the later rounds.

Tadhg's mind was buzzing.

I wonder if he knows this one in F?
What key does he do that one in?
I'll not go too fast yet, leave 'em hanging on later?
They'll not know these ones?

Weekends spent in the musical furnaces of Milltown Malbay, Tobercurry and Drumshanbo to name but three had him battle hardened.

O'Connell leaned over to Aidan.

"You get Lúnasa's latest CD yet? Track 3, fuckin' amazin'!"

"Aye right enough but you wanna hear Hayden playin' that one on the banjo, Jesus Murphy!" replied Aidan. "Here, do you know this one?"

Away he went, the bow carving an invisible musical statue in the air around him.

"Fuckin' right," said Ogee, straight in behind with the drum.

His style was something else, the multi tapping, skin bending, driving with your eyes closed artistry of youth. Youth and the experience of time well spent learning from master drummers like Belfast's Tomaí Lortay.

"Mighty lads! Yahoo!" roared Curran.

The serpent had bitten him right between the legs.

"Go'n to fuck," he shouted. "Pints!"

Then one by one like instrument laden eagles the others swooped in. Tones, sounds, strings, rhythms, toe tapping, pint swallowing, eyes closed, eyes open, heads up, heads down in a frenzy of what Ogee would term Death Trad. But there was nothing dead about it, this was life itself. Irish traditional musical ferocity in all its glory. In and out the sets of tunes breathed, resting then building but never stopping.

"Drive 'er," roared Tadhg, beyond his control.

It was an instinctive, primal gulder from the pit of his stomach. His turn to lead them round.

Which one? Which fuckin' tune? C'mon, think!

The wrong one would wreck the momentum.

Right ye fuckers.

"Splendid Isolation," shouted Tadhg. "G minor."

"Christ the night! He means business!" exclaimed O'Connell, quickly sliding his movable capo up the neck of his bouzouki.

He fired a look at Tadhg to say 'don't fuck this one up, it's too good'.

The serpent had them all now and they writhed in its grasp, mesmerised and mesmeric all at once. The air around the table spiralled up to the old white painted ceiling like a miniature tornado sucking in the emotions and souls of those present. Their bodies writhed and lurched according to the confines of their instruments. They had entered another place, the trad zone, where the music was all.

Then just like that the tune ended, the set was over with the sudden stop of silence. The walls of the bar took a breath.

No one spoke until Curran,

"Jesus fuck!" he roared. "Mighty tunes lads, mighty"

His eyes were wide in the sheer joy of it all. None of the others replied in words. Instead a look of mutual respect was shared. It was still fairly early, there was more to come.

Pete offered token applause and shook his head slowly in admiration. He was more of a Dire Straits man but appreciated talent when he heard it.

"Ye lads should be on the stage," came a voice.

The company looked up and regarded a small bearded man with a fiddle case.

"Can I join you?"

"Of course," answered Tadhg, happy to welcome another musical soul to the fray. This was special. Everyone was on form. He had played in too many sessions where the effort was there but the magic wasn't. It was here tonight and he was going to inhale deeply.

36. First Refusal

The little man proceeded to sit beside Pete, who on hearing the yell from Curran had headed barward and was returning with a tray of pints, on the house. A gesture not missed by the musicians who raised their glasses in turn to Peadar.

"All right?" he said, a common enough greeting.

"Yes great. I heard rumour of a tune tonight. Takes the heat off yourself Aidan eh?" he replied.

"Does John," grinned Aidan.

Aidan was the mainstay of the regular Friday night session and had been so for more years than he cared to recall. Come rain, hail or more hail or snow he'd be there in that corner pounding out jigs and reels and whatever else he could think of for at least three hours a night. He'd had many musical companions over the years but they tended to come and go. Of late Curran had been his partner and McManus's was all the better for it. They had formed another space for live traditional music to be played. A space into which John McEntee ventured often.

John had been one to whom the music had come late in life. A factory foreman by day he had watched several generations of workers move through the job. He had also watched over his ailing parents and having never married he was left as their main carer. This meant that a few tunes here and there were a treasure and something he enjoyed immensely. He quickly tuned up (by ear of course) and sat ready with his fiddle across his lap.

"Sure give us one there John," said Curran, momentarily lifting his nose from the pint glass.

"Ach Curran! Jesus! I'm only in. No. I'll listen in for a minute."

John knew better than to just start at the first request. He wasn't about to forego the etiquette of the newly arrived.

"Grand, do you know this one John?" asked Tadhg.

Tadhg began again, a little slower than before. The first few notes were greeted with an 'Ah lovely' from John for whom the tune was meant.

With this call and reply John had entered the first level of the session and he picked up his bow and met Tadhg at the end of the first part of the tune.

"What's that one?" asked Ogee.

"Fucked if I know," replied O'Malaigh.

The others in the circle held back to invite John in a little further. He stopped momentarily, quickly put the fiddle to his ear and plucked at the strings. Tadhg maintained rhythm and volume and eyed John carefully. In the same movement

John, having discerned that he in fact knew the tune had used the old move of false tuning to give him a moment to clear his head. He sensed Tadhg knew very well how to play and he didn't want to let himself down with early looseness.

He restruck the bow across the strings just as the tune turned again.

A loud 'G'won to fuck' spilled raucously from Curran's frothy lips and the circle was closed again with its new initiate. The briefest of smiles ran across Tadhg's eyes.

This fucker can play.

The mood of the bar now had moved to the place that only live traditional Irish music can bring stone, slate and wood. The door opened and several men entered unknowingly into this new atmosphere and were at once both surprised and excited. Monday pints were quiet affairs mostly where weekend states were relived along with the weather. This was different. This was the energy of years being administered knowingly from a circle of musicians. Tadhg felt it made the pints taste better. The head on the Guinness was whiter than before. The ebb and flow of the tune made the Carlsberg bubbles fizz all the harder. Fuck it even the crisps were crunchier.

"H'won horse!" grunted Ogee.

John had established himself now and was neck and neck with Tadhg as regards leading the set. He felt immediately at ease and welcome. The first tune had entered its fourth return and was now nearing the end.

Time for another. Ah sure I'll try it, thought John.

He quickly caught Tadhg's eye and raised his head a little as if to say 'follow me'.

All eyes fell on him for the second between the end of one tune and the start of another. John drew heavy and fast on the first note of the new tune.

Bang! The troupe moved with him. Smiles lit up faces and eyes gleamed and fired looks around the circle. The bridge had been beautifully gapped and away into it again they went, rhythms and hearts and fingers all in unison creating magic. From the bar came a very loud, "Yeehooo! This is gonna be some night."

37. Chicken burger loads

I wonder if anyone has died by being sat on? wondered Fr Dower.

He was attempting to make sense of the furore. Tea and cakes had miraculously appeared and soon the circle of missionary fathers was edging cream from their lips and avoiding crumbs as best they could.

The time was slipping by and he wondered should he not push on a little further.

"You know lads it has been wonderful to catch up with you all but I'd better go and see the aunt. She's not the best."

"Oh I am sorry to hear that Eugene. Now which aunt is that?" asked Fr Jonathan.

This was a risky strategy. Fr Jonathan Morgan was a small, bald and vociferous priest originally from Belfast. He loved debating and investigating any and all philosophical questions. Eugene knew that he was well in with the bishop and here he was revealing his cover story when there was really no need.

"Ah 'tis the mother's only sister, Geraldine. She's getting near the end and I thought I'd better call down."

No takers.

"Well Eugene, it was lovely to see you again. You could have picked a quieter day mind you but sure it makes for a good yarn," said Sean.

"Yes it does indeed."

He shook hands warmly with the assorted holy men. He had very fond memories of them and this place but more pressing matters were on his mind. He waved farewell and drove up the tree lined lane. As there was no sick aunt and it was too late to drive that much further he decided it easier all round if he checked in for the night in the town's grand hotel, the Canal Court.

Treat yourself.

It was now the crowning glory after the renovation of all the old storage buildings that lined Newry Canal. He collected his old suitcase and headed in through the front doors. He had a quiet smile to himself as the grand oak staircase that greeted him circled heavenward.

What a job they've done here.

He approached the attractive young lady behind the reception desk and inquired as to the possibility of a room for the night.

"Aye surely fa'r, no ba (Yes of course father, no bother)," she answered.

Ha, pure Newry. Love it.

"Thank you."

Up he went and sat on the large, crisply blanketed bed. His suitcase sat alongside. He was impatient. There were places to be.

"You can wait here. I'm away out."

No answer from the suitcase and he took that as agreement with his idea. The hotel shimmered all round him but as it was a Monday and the atmosphere was less frenetic than what one might expect on a weekend.

Newry waited outside.

The town, he thought. *Now they call you a city. You're as much a city as I am a champion of celibacy. Of course I really should be a champion of celibacy but you should not be a city.*

Opposite him now in the evening air the pink leaves of the cherry blossom trees that bordered the canal scattered themselves on the breeze. They reminded him of the confetti of the many weddings he'd administered.

Young love in bloom.

He turned left out of the hotel and strolled up to the crossroads. The canal stretched out silently before him before disappearing under the bi-county town hall, one half in Armagh and the other in Down, the only one in Ireland as far as he knew. It mirrored his inner divisions, especially these last days. Maggie was alive in his thoughts and standing beside him as he closed his eyes for a moment.

"You fancy a Friar Tuck?" he asked her.

She nodded silently and he walked toward Newry's version of McDonald's, KFC and Burger King.

Now spread high, wide and welcome at the top of Monaghan Street, he recalled its more humble beginnings as a small counter bar chippy.

Progress? Dunno. I wonder if the chicken burgers are still as good.

He walked along regarding more of the large store house buildings that once had housed grain and all manner of trade off the canal. Most now were restaurants and furniture stores. The traffic lights went about their colourful routine. The cars queued momentarily and on green were highly revved and away.

Fr Dower placed his order at the brightly lit and aroma rich counter. *Certainly there hasn't been a human invented yet that isn't whisked off to chip heaven by the odour of deep fat wonderfulness.* He gazed on the varied menu. Suddenly behind him he heard the many voiced crescendo that is a group of slightly intoxicated women.

He moved to one side and admired their shapely forms from a position of subtle advantage. He noticed too that they all carried various musical instruments and heard amongst the orders for burgers and chips phrases such as 'aye quer arse on him' 'what sort of a name's Tadhg?' 'I thought O'Malaigh was nice, he could squeeze my box anytime' and 'not sure about thon big hairy gilloot'.

Tadhg. The Pockel. The lads.

They also relayed, amongst orders for chicken boxes, chicken burgers with loads of coleslaw and subsequent guilt at eating them which then got 'aw fuck its', that they too were bound for west Cork.

38. Breather

Fingers whizzed around their respective instruments like bees dancing directions on the hive to some wondrous nectar. Each one independent and yet part of the musical mission that now consumed the bar. McManus's was hopping. Reel followed reel, unspoken changes between tunes and keys. The crescendo of this particular set had one man at the bar leaping about like a tribe's shaman, all vowels and contortions.

"G'won lads. Jaysus, that's the stuff."

The pints flowed, appearing on the table as if by magic. Sometimes they made their way from the bar via a sea of hands like food via Trócaire volunteers. Sometimes a pair of arms would lean in with the white tips of the Guinness delicately peering over the edge of the glass. It was mostly Guinness at first, the black fuel of Ireland and beyond. Each pint was a work of art, poetry in a pint glass. Well, at least until the lads wrapped their lips around them at which point they became another of many martyrs.

"You boys should be in a band. That's fierce stuff altogether," came a voice.

It was Delaney. He was a builder with fingers on him like bunny rabbits. He was in the pub every night. No work in the country worth a damn but always a pound for a pint.

"Ye can keep your Three Danaans and Lúnacy and all that. That's powerful lads…deadly."

"You mean De Danaan? Ye fuckin' balloon," replied Pádraig.

"Aye well sure there's about six of them on the go at the minute. Those lads can play. Here I'll manage yiz sure. Christ we'll make a fortune."

If he ever saw another trowel it'd be too soon.

Tadhg heard the offer alright and at that moment a manager a la Brian Epstein sounded great.

Of course Delaney had a fair point, the lads could play and play well. The fact was that they didn't have the desire or discipline to take the show on the road. Each had been in a band or three growing up and indeed would do a few days here or there with any touring group that might ask. This did happen occasionally and Tadhg was always grateful for the money that came with it. But for him a band meant rehearsals, meeting up, being sensible. It also meant hard bloody work. He sometimes struggled with the playing for big crowds one night in Germany and rapturous applause and the next night doing a session in town with no one listening and the bloody TV on at the same time.

As he often heard 'the gig's the easy bit, 'tis the fuckin' getting there's the problem.' Still, Tadhg thought it was nice to hear that someone thought the music was good.

Someday maybe.

"Aye right big lad, what's your percentage?" he shouted up at Delaney.

"Ha, fifty percent of everything except the drinks bill. You fuckers get a hundred percent of that."

"Aye shove it up yer hole," roared Cullen. "Get a few pints in be more like ye!"

Delaney retired from the conversation with a smile. No world tour on the horizon this month. He nodded at Pádraig and the order for the table was duly made.

Fuckin' trowel, he thought.

The players drew breath and the instruments were put to one side. This was the session version of the interval. Time for a yarn and a wee dander. Being a Monday night there were students from the local college out and about. Instinctively Ogee and O'Malaigh's bat like hearing for the fairer sex had picked up soft tones giggling from next door. O'Connell and McLynn stayed put on the promise of a status report from the lads.

"Here, just taking a wee scout 'round. Back in a minute," said Ogee.

The two lads squeezed out past knees, tables, pints and instruments. Tadhg placed his fiddle in the little alcove at the bottom of the window as did Aidan. "Ye like a bit a Hayden then Aidan?" said Tadhg.

He could hear the master Tyrone fiddler in Aidan's style.

"Aye I do, he's lethal."

"He is. Here, have ye ever met Gino?"

"Ha, the bodhrán player? No I haven't but I hear he's powerful craic," replied Aidan reaching for his pint.

"Mighty altogether. Good bloody singer too. But like, he's really good on the drum. I used to not hear it or to be honest wasn't listening but I saw him one night there and he knows what he's at."

"Well if ye're playing with that outfit ye'd need to. O'Connor, Hayden, Dónal Murphy, Doherty and a sprinkling of Arty McGlynn. Sure it's like the Carlsberg trad band."

Mini conversations began around the table, mysterious to the outsider but pure session banter.

Subjects on the acquisition of good rosin, the price of bouzouki strings, instrument makers (some better than others), sets of tunes, key changes, old recordings, Sligo style flute, Donegal fiddlers, festivals in Teelin, Carrick and the like. John took a healthy swig from his pint and savoured the moment. He loved it when new tunes got a run out. He loved the session each week but this was different, something new.

"Anybody seen Pete?" asked O'Connell.

He had slipped out in the furore and there were *four* empty pint glasses just where he was sitting.

39. Meeting Nan Rice and friends

Eugene let the girls order their grub. He quickly ate his chicken burger, rubbing the extra coleslaw off his lips with the back of his hand. He'd never do that in the parochial house. Newry whizzed by outside the large chip and fizzy pop decorated windows.

I wonder if it's still there?

He was thinking of Nan Rice's bar, in its day the place for traditional music in Newry town. Of course many other fine sessions played out in the surrounding countryside toward Mayobridge and Hilltown but Nan's was his favourite.

He put an inch in his step back along the canal and quickly made it to the pub's old front door he'd so often pushed open. It yielded without trouble and the granite ridged floor slabs stretched out like Finn McCool's draught board. The bar was long and narrow and stretched away to the promise of greater things. He followed it round. Many great sessions had happened down in these alcoves. He could hear them still. The laughter at jokes, the ferocity of the music, the lilt of the recitation and the grace of the song. The walls had stored them for him.

"Ah my God," he said. "They were the nights."

"You still talking to yourself you oul bollox?" came a voice.

Eugene turned round slowly to face his accuser, although the voice was all at once familiar.

"You still getting lost in your back garden?" he quipped back.

"Ha, indeed I am. How the hell are ye?"

It was Petesy Quinn, a retired school master and a man of boundless enthusiasm for life, county Down football, the outdoors, writing and traditional music.

"I'm doing grand Petesy. I was just in memory lane there. You mind the nights here?"

"Jesus I do Eugene, they were powerful weren't they?"

"Aye they were…they were indeed."

"What brings you to Newry? It's been ages since I saw you and if I might add you're even uglier now than the last time."

"Ah now Petesy 'tis a long story but here, will ye have a pint?"

"I'll have two if you're able!"

The order was made and the two men sat down at the now quiet session table. For Eugene it was an emotional moment. He had been here often with Maggie.

Petesy and his girlfriend would make a four and they'd lap up the craic like nobody's business.

"There were some great sessions around then Petesy. What's the story these days?"

"Ye'd hardly get a tune in the town now but for Beyonce and the like."

"Aye... feast or famine. Ye mind the singing session out the road there?" asked Eugene.

"Of course. I mind you murdering Raglin Road many's the night."

"Yer arse, they just couldn't find my key."

"What key was that? Z?"

They laughed together and nosed into their drinks.

The singing session at the Cove Bar was indeed something. All manner of song, poem, speech and occasional marriage proposal was heard. The words mattered there. The tunes were played too but singers found a warm welcome and a place to air their feelings via compositions self-written or classic.

"Serious good order. She got better order than the priest and I should know," smiled Eugene.

"She did. Here did ye ever make it back to Peter Doran's?"

"Jesus I didn't. Another great house for music," replied Petesy.

Doran's was possibly the smallest session room in Ireland. The pub itself was an old house converted for drinking purposes. Many swore the room was designed for fairies but it didn't stop them squeezing in of a Saturday night. Not only did they squeeze in of course but they managed remarkably to squeeze into the same seat each time and if that wasn't synchrony enough they sang the same songs in the same order too. Indeed a new song was treated with the wonder of the second coming and mistrust in equal portion.

"Ha do you mind the night oul' Jemmy sang that song?"

"I do," answered Eugene.

Of course oul' Jemmy sang a song every night but on this occasion he ventured something new, something that meant breathing in a different place in a line.

"Sure wasn't he going great guns until he had to draw a long breath and on the inhale managed to loosen the top row of delph."

Eugene nearly choked on his pint.

"The cratur caught them just before they landed in the neighbour's brandy."

"He finished the song though! Then put the teeth back," said Petesy.

"The least he could do. Don't think he sang it for another ten years," laughed Eugene.

The pints quickly disappeared amid reminiscences of the old days around the then many musical session bars of Newry and District. Eugene didn't want to give away too much and steered clear of any avenues of conversation that might be awkward.

"So what has you down anyway?" asked Petesy.

"The Lord...works in mysterious ways," smiled back Eugene. "Church business, you know the usual stuff. Speaking of same, 'tis time I got this bag of bones back to the hotel? Are ye heading that way?"

"Aye, no bother."

The two old friends finished off their pints and said their goodbyes to Nan's.

"You ever think of Maggie at all?" asked Petesy.

Eugene smiled and looked at him straight in the eye.

"More than you'll ever know, Petesy, more than you'll ever know."

40. Hidden Depths

It began just out of sight of the table, a low and musical voice with a sweetness and calmness to it that contrasted starkly with the previous frenzy. The numerous heads turned helplessly toward the singer and the song.

"Shhhhh!" belted Pádraig.

His initial command was largely ignored in the curiosity and fervour of the room.

"SHHHHH!" he said again with an element of threat.

The lads still in situ at the table leaned over and strained to see from whence and from whom the voice came.

Silence now almost complete in the wee bar save for the door dulled chatter of next door's crowd who were oblivious to the turn of events.

"On a Monday mornin' early…" sang the voice.

Fuck, thought Tadhg. '*The Boys of Mullach Bán…the old country!*'

"My wandering steps did lead me…"

His mind now raced to recall nights in 'The Stray Leaf', the world's greatest folk club. Bottles by the neck and seating comprising of beer kegs, DIY benches, bottle crates and all manner of chair all under corrugated tin and walls thick enough to hide a Mini Metro. The musical annex of O'Hanlon's bar.

"Down by a farmer's station through meadows and green lawn…"

The people in the bar were now rapt and held silence. It was instinctive. A song like this demanded respect and needed to be sung. It was one of the big songs.

Who the fuck?

Tadhg stood up to see the singer. It was Pete.

Jesus!

Whatever his perceptions of Pete there was no denying the big lad could sing. Every line delivered as if he was at the writing of the song itself.

"I heard great lamentation…"

Tadhg now joined in. He knew he was no singer but he didn't care. Certain songs just pull you along anyway…though not too loudly of course. Others made singing noises too under the radar, musical hums and half words.

"The wee birds they were warbling…"

Pete had slipped off to a wee nook just to the left of the bar on a small seat so that only the top of his cropped head was easily visible. The shock of such beautiful words coming out of him inspired the company. Indeed, a few more voices now joined in.

"We'll have no more engagements with the boys of Mullach Bán."

The end of the first verse. Pete inhaled and in perfect rhythm began again. This time to a few 'good mans' and 'g'wans'.

The walking gonad brothers that were O'Malaigh and Ogee timed their return like the session veterans they were. Between the last word and the first of the next verse they had rejoined the circle, grinning widely. Ogee shot over a wink to McLynn and O'Connell.

Skirt identified and targeted.

The only noises other than the singer were the occasional car humming past the door and the hiss of Guinness as it decorated yet another glass in blackness.

There was now a feeling of camaraderie in the bar. For the present they were all boys from Mullach Bán exiled from their beloved and beloved country.

"But now we are endangered
By a vile deceiving stranger
Who has ordered deportation
For the Boys of Mullach Bán."

They all knew of the stranger in the song and each felt the pain of the words in their own memories of recent history. But like many's another song the bitterness, anger, sadness they felt remained within the verses. Different times now. Better times ahead.

The poor fucker with the mobile phone had no chance. The ear cursing bleepity bleep bleep began suddenly and threatened to puncture the whole mood. Pádraig was swift to act.

"Get that fuckin' thing off or I'll break your fuckin' neck!" he whispered with an 'I'll also eat your children' stare.

Pete ploughed on.

He's done this before, thought Tadhg.

Such a distraction might have derailed a less experienced performer. The phone was silenced. One more verse to go.

"To end my lamentation we're all in consternation…"

The finish line was in sight and the breathing became less fraught but only in preparation. The climax was building.

"For want of education I here must end my song…"

Several glasses were gripped tightly raised to mouths in readiness.

"Who cares for recreation without consideration…"

Tadhg readied the bow. If ever there was a time to rebirth a session it was surely approaching. The others prepared their instruments, tapping strings deathly carefully for tuning. The voice slowed and drew out the last line and in accordance with the scriptures spoke the last few words.

"We're sent for transportation from the…hills of Mullach Bán."

Well if the roar that went up didn't nearly blow the windows clean out onto the road. It might as well have been the winning goal at Croke Park.

"C'mon ta fuuuck!" yelled Cullen.

Pádraig stood transfixed behind the bar, the pride and passion of it all hitting him like Mike Tyson's elbow. Clapping, back slapping 'get that man a drink' 'powerful' 'fucked if I'm workin' the marra' and the like bounced around in the aftermath.

The time had come. Tadhg shook and cracked open a reel, swiftly followed by the ever ready Ogee and one by one the lads turned the wheel into the next level of chaos. Another roar. Cullen was so happy he felt like shitting in his pants right there. Pádraig smiled again. This was indeed some Monday night.

41. Out on the Ocean

"By the way," asked McLynn mid tune. "Where the fuck are we stayin' the night?"

"Don't you worry yourself," replied Cullen. "There's a room or two upstairs for just such occasions."

"Sweet to the beat," laughed Ogee.

Not a note missed by anyone but it was a precursor to decline. The pints which had magically enhanced proceedings knew well that they would be wreaking havoc shortly. The difficulty for musicians, well for some musicians anyway, is knowing when to ease up, to let the stallion have a break. Tadhg, though an experienced jockey in many ways hadn't quite sussed the off switch.

"Laphroaig!" roared O'Malaigh.

No sooner said than down they came, seven little glasses with their swirling golden content, Islay single malt Scotch whisky. The smell of peat out of them would near take your eyebrows off.

"Goodnight Irene," shouted O'Connell.

Fuck it, thought Tadhg. *This probably is a mistake. Ah what the fuck.*

The glasses rattled on the table with a hearty thud as each came down. Job done.

Another round of tunes followed but this time Tadhg had to concentrate a little harder on what he was doing. He became aware of the movements his fingers were making. The bow felt heavy. He found now that he was thinking about notes. He was aware of his foot tapping, his breathing and most tellingly, he felt the skin behind his ears begin to tighten again. He was nearing the height of his arc. The firework effect had almost arrived and he set down his bow and sat back in his seat. The others continued to launch into reel after reel.

Fuckers, how do they do it? Breather time. C'mon ye'll be grand.

"You OK horse?" asked Ogee. "You're looking a bit green about the gills there?"

Tadhg had to think how to reply. The words were queuing up on his tongue pushing to get out.

"Aye great, fine, yip. No borr! Portugal nil Norn Iron five!" he shouted like a demented Jackie Fullerton. The last outburst accompanied with the pointing arm actions of a prancing Michael Flatley and latterly hijacked by a certain Usain Bolt.

"Fuck sake you're full ye cunt," laughed Ogee.

"Full my hole. I'm just getting my second wind."

Second wind or not the night was getting shorter by the minute for Tadhg. However, he did pull round a bit and was aware of proceedings, aware enough to think about some place to sleep other than under the table…or worse.

"Here, Cullen ye bastard. What's the craic for a kip? Can we sleep here? Did you not say they had a room upstairs or something?"

"Aye you're grand. I had a word with Pádraig there. If you're fucked give him a nod and he'll give ye a key. But 'tis early yet. Here Pádraig throw us down a brandy."

With that bridge now crossed brandy suddenly seemed like a wondrous way to continue. Any thoughts of Baltimore could wait. Down came the glowing hazel drops and quickly disappeared into the dark gullets of the willing. Musically, the night had reached its zenith some time before. The tunes had lost a little of their fizz and eyes strayed to watches and thoughts of a Tuesday morning in Dundalk. Slowly the punters unbuckled themselves from the ride. The five hour roller coaster had pulled in for the night.

"Ah Christ lads that was fierce music. Fair play."

It was mobile phone man, in hope of redemption.

The outside door to the wee bar now let in the fresh night air and it clashed harshly with Tadhg's well tanked perceptions. He breathed it in all the same. It was a reminder of the world…and chips. The air was strong with the smell of boiling fat.

"Ah here, any of you fuckers want a burger?" asked Pete.

"Ah fuck aye," answered Cullen. "Who's going?"

"I'll go sure. There's a chipper round the corner," offered Pete, who was really being quite sensible. He smiled and put on his coat and got clearance from Pádraig with a shout of 'grub time, back in five'.

42. Bed and Buckfast

Ogee and O'Malaigh had returned to the promise of women next door leaving Cullen, Aidan, Tadhg, John, O'Connell, and McLynn around the table. This was the wind down. The madness of earlier was now replaced with a settling. Not unlike the miraculous events that occur in every pint of Guinness.

"Are ye about for a day or two?" asked John, keen to do it all again.

"Ha, no mate. We're for down the road," replied O'Connell.

"Where to?"

"Em? Where are we goin' Tadhg?"

"Baltimore."

Tadhg's tongue climbed over every syllable like a snail on a mushroom assault course.

"Fiddle Fair?"

"That's the one," laughed O'Connell.

"Ah lads, ye'll have the craic. I was never at it but I hear 'tis great," said John.

"Sure why don't ye come with us?" asked O'Connell, with little thought for the practicalities of a positive answer.

"No, no I'll not make it this time but sure ye'll maybe call in on your way back?"

John put away his fiddle as he spoke and was soon shaking hands in fond farewell. He headed out into the night.

"Nice player Aidan," said Tadhg, slowly coming back from deep water.

"Aye, good man too. He be's in most Fridays. Loves the tunes altogether."

"Sure, ye'll be for Baltimore yourself Aidan?" asked O'Connell.

"Will I fuck. I'd love to, don't get me wrong but I've too much goin' on…ye know. Time I wasn't here."

Slowly and carefully Aidan put away his fiddle. The white haired, dark slender wooded bow he handled as if replacing Excalibur into the stone. Aware that his delicacy was drawing attention he turned and smiled.

"Ye can't be too careful. Sure at the All Ireland last year some hallion sat on my bastardin' fiddle! I only popped out for a smoke and come back to see fuckin' strings and pegs everywhere."

Tadhg winced at the thought. It was of course the ultimate disaster for any musician.

"Jesus! What did you do?" asked Tadhg.

"Sure what could I do? The useless shite that did it was lyin' pole axed and half the place trying to lift him out. I had a look around me and said 'fuck it' and got clean stocious for the next three days."

He closed up his case and also bade them farewell.

Pete met him at the door and they shook hands. He sat down at the table with a big brown bag of deeply fried everything. Chips, burgers, chicken, dip, hot dogs…

"Here c'mon, get tore in," he said.

The lads didn't need much encouragement and soon the contented silence of burger eating filled the air.

"Lads, there's a room upstairs. Ye are welcome to it. Don't wreck the place and we'll be alright. Here Pete, there's the key," said Pádraig who left them and was heard bellowing out 'drink up please' in the other bar.

"See yiz in the mornin'? What time we away?" asked Ogee.

Apparently both he and O'Malaigh had touched for two women.

"Be here at ten or ye can fuckin' walk," replied Pete.

"Right, g'luck, that'll do."

"Fuck them two would get up on the crack in a plate," said McLynn.

He stuck his hand deep into his coat.

"In the absence of women there's always this…Lurgan Champagne."

The dark but brightly yellow labelled bottle was raised like the Statue of Liberty's torch. The lads headed to bed with the sweet taste of Buckfast wet on their lips.

43. The Road South

"Well well!" exclaimed Pete, tucking into his bacon buttie. "Men of your word or what?"

Ogee and O'Malaigh approached the 'Tasty Bite' café breakfast table where the lads had been recounting last night's fun.

"Did ye get yer hole?" asked McLynn.

He would've been jealous but his head was too sore.

"G'way to fuck. A policeman wouldn't ask ye that," answered Ogee with a grin.

"Jammy hurs," added O'Connell. "My arse feels like the Japanese flag."

"Aye I smelt ye this mornin'. Ye must a been shittin' pure silage," said Tadhg.

"I should sell it," replied O'Connell.

"Na you wouldn't have a chance. Mine has that extra consistency. The farmers' friend. Like Mr Whippy ice cream only…better. Sausages," added Pete quite seriously.

"Sausages?" asked O'Malaigh with one on the end of his fork.

"Aye, great for shite. Keeps me right anyway," answered Pete, eating one in a single bite.

Tadhg looked at Pete and while he might have been regular he had a gut on him like a balloon full of piss.

"Aye, the fuckin' Sausage Diet, that'll be the next big one," he said sarcastically.

"Here I'm tellin' ye smart arse," laughed Pete. "Time we weren't here."

They had had a fair night's sleep in the wee room above the bar. A mattress each and a sleeping bag proved more than adequate.

"So, how'd ye get on?" asked McLynn again.

"Put it this way, all that glitters isn't fuckin' gold," replied O'Malaigh.

"Go on…"

"Right we went back to their flat and had a few beers and a jay or two. All goin' well 'til the next thing fuckin' alarms start goin' off everywhere."

"Fire alarms?"

"No, dopey. Fuckin' question alarms! Aye of course, ye twat. Turns out there was a flat full of ones from Sweden or somewhere downstairs and their fuckin' fireplace went on fire. We're lucky to get out at all."

"Ha! So what happened?"

"Ach the fire brigade pulled up and evacuated everyone. So there's us on the street like dickheads and the two women bleating about clothes and TVs and DVDs and fuckin' make up and shit."

"You wankers," added Tadhg sympathetically.

"But here all's well that ends well. Fire out without much bother and all back in. So like the two were in a fair state of shock so we had to apply first aid…you know," winked Ogee.

"Several times," laughed O'Malaigh.

"Away to fuck. Yiz are havin' a laugh?" said McLynn.

They left the café, re-entered the car and were on their way through the early Dundalk streets in no time.

"Believe what ye like. They said to come back anytime," laughed Ogee.

Much wind was passed what with beer, late chips, Buckfast and a fried breakfast. All windows were down and the wind howled about the car. The fresh air revived them all and the mood was good.

The new motorway to Dublin stretched out before them and was a sight to behold. Pete was of an age to recall the arduous journey that Dundalk to Dublin used to be. Arduous in that the roads weren't great, all gears and traffic lights. He also remembered enjoying little streets in wee road towns like Dunleer and Castlebellingham. Indeed there was a bar there he always called in on when passing through. Different now though. No time for detours. He had a quick hoke in the glove compartment and pulled out a cassette tape.

"Here put that on Tadhg."

Tadhg took a look at the artist.

"John Campbell… 'On the Hip of Sliabh Gullion'."

"A classic. Fuck me Pete, you're a man after my own heart."

"Who is it?" asked Ogee, tapping his fingers rhythmically off his knee caps.

"Who is it? It's only the greatest story teller that ever lived, that's who," answered Tadhg.

"Aye, who?"

"John Campbell."

"The Rhinestone Cowboy man?"

"That's Glen Campbell ye tool," snapped Pete. "Here, I'll let him do the talking"

The tape slotted noisily into its player and began. The strains of a broad Mullach Bán accent slowly filled the car capturing hungover ears in its web. For the next forty minutes the lads listened like school children and laughed aloud at regular intervals. The road was swallowed up with tales of Clinton the Vet, Peter go Slap, water hens and wangs. Pete glimpsed at the rapt faces through his rear-view mirror and revelled in the power of the skilled seanachie. Tadhg remembered hearing this tape many times and had been lucky enough to see Campbell himself live. He laughed again until his sides were sore.

44. Dublin

The long hems of Dublin city stretched north and covered places like Swords, Malahide and Drumcondra to name but three. Tadhg whispered them slowly and lamented. Each name originated in the Gaelic language but now their meanings just echoed sadly in their English versions. He leaned his head against the window so that his vision blurred with the movement of the car.

Dublin.

He was not as regular a visitor to the capital as he would have liked although he was proud to call many 'Dubs' close friends. Indeed he was aware that there were cousins somewhere on the north side.

Blanchardstown, he thought, but he hadn't seen them since God knows when.

"Ye ever meet the Beaumont Express?" asked McLynn

"The what?" asked Pete.

"Yes, I know him well," said Ogee. "Absolutely lethal banjo player, guitar player and singer and proud republican. And he's about eight foot six! I did a wee turn with him on Fuerte Ventura a couple of years ago."

"What about him?" asked Tadhg, intrigued.

"He's a martyr for the craic," said Ogee.

"He is," confirmed McLynn. "We should give him a shout."

"Where does he live?" asked Pete, fearing another mystery tour.

"Gogarty's, Temple Bar," said McLynn.

"Ha, he lives in a pub? Perfect. I like him already," said Tadhg.

"No not really but he runs the sessions there. What time is it?"

"'Tis half one, Tuesday afternoon," replied Pete, who really wanted to say Star Date 2215.2 in the fashion of James T Kirk.

"They'll be kickin' off a wee downstairs session at two. What do you say Pete? We'll just say hello and go on…promise."

Pete looked at him in a way that meant it would just be a quick stop.

Gogarty's sat on the corner of one of the crossroads of very busy little streets that filter through Temple Bar. The bustle of the place was intense; tourists, shoppers, Dubs all going about their business at breakneck pace.

The lads ambled slowly to the double doors and noticed a table on their immediate right with fiddles and flutes already in situ. The smell of food was almost over powering. Big healthy slabs of gravy covered beef, ham and roasties steaming under the heating lights at the bar. As musicians they all cast an eye at the table and were received with not hostility but more a 'this is our place' look from those seated there. Territory and protection of instruments the reason, not unreasonable in a city where the light fingered often plied their trade.

All seats filled and even at the relatively early hour of two the place was jammed. This would not be a session they would be playing in.

"Pints?" asked Tadhg.

"Aye go on," answered Ogee, speaking for all.

"Red Bull for me," said Pete.

The lads stood at the bar as McLynn chatted with one of the musicians at the table. He'd spent a fair bit of time in Dublin at college and knew a lot of the local heads. As he wished them all the best the longest form that any of them had ever seen came in the door.

"Fuck," said Tadhg.

"McLynn ye bollox. How's de craic? Ah Jaysus, Ogee!" said the giant.

"Ach Sean just passing through. How ye goin'?" replied McLynn.

"Deadly. Here are ye staying for tunes?"

"Not sure…c'm 'ere and say hello."

McLynn did the introductions.

"Lads this is the Beaumont Express himself, Seanie Lynch."

Handshakes and 'howrye's' followed. All eyes looked up to Seanie. The trad scene does not have many very tall people, it has fewer very tall and talented people. Big Seanie was one. He had a singing voice like Ronnie Drew after two nights on the rip and could play the banjo like Jimi Hendrix and Animal from the Muppets mixed.

"Here, 'tis a bit mad here I know a wee place," he suggested.

All eyes meandered towards Pete.

"Where?" he asked.

"The Cobblestone, just ten minutes away," answered Seanie.

Pete agreed. No one had any instruments out with them. What could go wrong? They sculled their pints and followed the big lad out the door.

"Ye playin' the night Seanie?" asked McLynn.

The others followed a step or two back.

"I am but not 'til nine. 'Tis a bit like work you know but it pays the bills."

Gogarty's was a bit of a conundrum among trad players. On the one hand the standard of the musicians and quality of the music was second to none but on the other it had become more of a show than a session, particularly upstairs. It was geared at the visiting clientele and they flocked to it. The ballads held their own and more here. The trad heads tended to play in the Cobblestone and McNeill's where they were 'on stage' in that they were in a session but not on a stage behind microphones.

"Aye, sure goodwill never paid the fuckin' electric yet," said Ogee.

In no time they had left the tempest of Temple Bar and were in the quieter surrounds of Stoneybatter. The bar welcomed them in with a whisper. They were the only ones there.

"Ye never would think this was Dublin at all," said O'Connell.

The previous pint had restored his vocal chords and he felt slightly less awful. So much so that he ventured barward.

"Howrye Seanie," said the grey haired, middle aged bundle of Dublin that was the barman.

"Tom, give these fuckers a pint will ye?" said Seanie.

Without asking, Tom had two glasses underneath two Guinness taps and both were filling immediately (hissity hiss bloody delicious hiss). The door opened again and several punters entered. The old bar was being reborn once more.

"Red Bull for me please," said Pete.

They sat round down at the corner where the session is held. Tadhg surveyed the many pictures and posters and felt at home. The walls had soaked up many sounds over the years. Tadhg strained to hear them.

"Great spot," he said.

"'Tis. Ye are for the Fiddle Fair I hear," said Seanie.

"We are indeed. Under the big lad's guidance," said Tadhg saluting Pete.

"Ha, ye'll have the craic down there. I'll be down on the Saturday all bein' well."

That could be interestin', thought Tadhg.

Behind them the door opened and the bang of instrument cases coming through a small doorway meant one thing. The afternoon session was about to begin.

45. Vultures

As can happen in any city the relative calm of an empty bar can and does change with amazing alacrity. The hiss of Guinness was now replaced with pre session energy. The four new arrivals carried banjo, fiddle, pipes and flute into the corner. They placed them out in preordained positions and quickly called a round.

"Tro' us a rown' der Tom, le do thoil," said the piper.

Tadhg noticed a peculiar twang to his accent. It was Dublin extra. But extra what?

German? Austrian? Russian? No, 'tis definitely German.

"Howrye Seanie, ye big bollox," said the piper.

"Howrye ye Alli?"

"Don't often see you over dis vay. Gogo's let ye out for good behaviour?" he teased.

"Seanie," said the flute player in greeting with a slight nod.

"Hi Seanie," smiled the girl with the fiddle.

Gradually the lads took their places at the table. Instruments now in hand and tuning pegs were twisted to meet at that wondrous invisible point inside the ear. The big half German, half Dubliner cursed liberally. All pipers are subject to the whim of their instrument and like a sleeping elephant they took a gentle awakening.

The lads at the bar listened intently but did not really acknowledge the warm up. They would suss things out before revealing any particular interest. Tadhg of course strained to hear the fiddler. She was lovely too with shoulder length dark hair and green eyes. He thought he detected a northern twang to her accent.

So many women!

He noticed that the fiddle itself was different from normal in that it had no cut-aways on either side. It was round not unlike a slightly overweight Marilyn Monroe.

Hmm, class looking.

In a matter of minutes the bar had a healthy crowd spread around the bar. Tom nipped this way and that filling pint glasses. Seanie and Ogee chatted briefly but soon the conversation stopped. The piper blasted off with something straight from a Bothy Band LP. The others were straight in behind.

"Starting with the classics," smiled O'Connell out of earshot.

"The oul' Kesh," whispered McLynn, referring to the tune's title.

Fuck, thought Tadhg. *This lad's right on the money.*

For a non-native this was some going, particularly on the pipes. Something seems to be missing when visitors play traditional music, not this guy. Tadhg guessed that he'd been here for some time with the accent and all. He'd obviously been listening.

"G'won," shouted O'Malaigh.

That was it. He had blown their cover but he didn't care. The travellers shared a smile. They knew this stuff. They had done a similar job last night. They were fully paid up members of Ireland's greatest gift to the world, the trad musicians club.

Whether from playing in Comhaltas competitions or whether by simple human nature, the competitive element in them was beginning to surface. They were 'Nordies' after all; that strange kind of half breed, half lunatic from the land beyond Dundalk. To be fair most in the South cared little for the border and welcomed all musicians from anywhere. However, there was always that little edge to such meetings and the lads were definitely the away team. As if to raise the stakes the flute player proceeded to play a reel that began familiarly enough but soon became a study in gymnastic jazz dexterity. A gauntlet of sorts you might say.

"Has any one seen the tune?" said McLynn, not one for Jazz.

"Well, as the mother would say ye have to applaud good play from whatever side," replied O'Malaigh.

The situation immediately diffused with one of his most effervescent 'yahoos'. Job done, smiles all round and an invitation.

"Ye lads got your weapons?" said Alli.

He had noticed the hungry look of circling musicians.

Pete shifted a little uncomfortably in his chair. He knew what was coming.

"We do and we don't, if you know what I mean," replied McLynn.

"Oi havvin' a clew watcha meen?" laughed Alli. "You're velcome to join us dough." And there it was, the open door. But they had no key, at least not yet anyway. Pete decided it was his moment.

"Look lads, we have a five hour journey ahead at least. I'm not staying in Dublin tonight no harm to anybody. I'm goin' after this one. Anyone that's for Cork would need to be ready. This shit ain't happenin' today."

It was a fair point. They all knew it. Perhaps the decision would have been impossible had they had their instruments but they did not. The big lad wasn't a bit slow.

"Ach the computer says no. We're for the Fiddle Fair," answered Tadhg.

"Ah deadly," said Alli. "I'll fuckin' see ye der. I'm headin' dowin on Tursde loyk."

"Right, we'll meet up sure," said Ogee, tapping his fingers prodigiously on the bar.

"We will," smiled Alli.

The lads finished their drinks, bade Seanie farewell and were played out the door by a rake of lightning fast reels. Tadhg hated leaving any session but this one nearly pulled the guts out of him.

"Right, c'mon. Down the road," he said and walked on keenly ahead of the others.

46. Roadside Stops

Eugene slept like the dead and woke like a zombie, all eyes and groans. He stretched as long as he could under the sheets. He hadn't slept so well for a long time. Perhaps it was the few pints or the lateness of the hour but his mind had settled after all the activity and anxiety of previous days. He had a healthy breakfast and looked out the window at the Canal, still water. The sun shone in on him and for a time at least he was in a good place. He had changed out of his priestly black garb and was in jeans and a light blue shirt so that to anyone looking on, a middle aged man of no particular consequence would fill their eyes. It's a peculiar thing to see a priest out of uniform. The light swallowing darkness of the attire brings its own dignity and gravitas. It's often the first line of a conversation without having to say a word. Eugene felt free. Free of its import and duty. He was a single man, God notwithstanding. He had things to do.

He settled up his bill for the room and was soon following in the lads' raucous footsteps. Unknown to him they were deliberating on the consistencies of human manure as he passed by Dundalk. He made good progress and paid his Euro toll at Drogheda. He liked Drogheda. Yes it was famously the public resting place of a dead man's head but more than that it had the shop and pub crammed streets that make Ireland such a remarkable place. It was a bigger cousin to Carlingford.

He wouldn't be stopping by today though, Oliver Plunkett would have to wait. It was fair drive to west Cork and he had many miles to cover before night. He remarked on the flat country side around him. Hardly a hill or mountain worth the name and it sat like a great green lake with the wind shaping small waves here and there.

Ireland's fall and rise, he thought.

He had driven the old road many times before and tapped the top of his gear stick in remembrance. It was seldom used between Newry and Dublin now. He'd seen the time his hand wouldn't be off it, negotiating small busy streets, tractors, livestock and who knew what else.

He was now approaching Dublin and the sound of Michael Coleman's fiddle playing filled his car via Raidió na Gaeltachta. The Sligo master was one of the first men to be recorded playing Irish traditional music on fiddle and had laid a deep furrow where many had tried to follow. Eugene had heard several of his recordings as a lad growing up. His father would occasionally play them and that was a grand affair. The neighbours would often come round to marvel not only at Coleman but that he had been captured to play forever on a large vinyl disc. They would be enthralled at the old gramophone and the clicks and scrapes of the needle. It was black and white music in his mind to match the old photographs of the young Coleman with fiddle under his chin and bow at the ready.

Music in colour didn't really begin until the seventies. Tommy Peoples, Frankie Gavin and Kevin Burke to name but three blasted fiddle music from Donegal to Düsseldorf, Darwin to Derry. He loved listening to them all when he could find the time. Prayers had taken a lot of time off him and he regretted it now.

Ye can't play a prayer on the fiddle, he often thought.

He fumbled amongst his cds, trying not to go over the ditch as his eyes flicked from cd cover to road and back.

Too risky.

He pulled in and found the one he wanted – 'The Master's Touch' by Seán Maguire.

Typical Maguire title but by God the carnaptious oul divil could play.

Onward to the fling of the bow and the Liffey banks.

47. The Wesht's a Wake

Their journey became a study in the ebbing of energy. The buzz of the session got them all to the car and away down the road. Dublin began to shrink around their shoulders and was quickly replaced with countryside, lots of countryside. The Belfast lads as a rule did not see too many trees and pastures. That's not to say Belfast isn't green. Indeed many would argue it was half orange too but that's another story. The city is like a bowl surrounded by mountains on one side and the Irish Sea on the other, both barrier and gateway.

Belfast life is all on the streets, fast paced, loud, brash, confident and ready for anything. The long shadow of anxiety had slowly lifted and revealed a treasure for the world to enjoy. A rough diamond perhaps, but one that the artisans of the city were polishing with great gusto.

This car load of piss artisans was in no state to polish anything. Fatigue had set in. They had stopped long enough for their bodies to relax and once on that road it's Hellish hard to get back. One by one they began to fall asleep. Heads fell onto shoulders and drool and other globules emanated from nostrils and mouth edges. Faces fell into the contortions of gravity and guards were stood down. Snores and deep breathing filled the back seat. Tadhg was jealous. He often had difficulty sleeping. Even though his eyes were sore and his body done he stayed with it and his thoughts danced on his head (mostly the self chastising types wondering what he was staying awake for).

"What's wrong, you're not sleepin'?" asked Pete, enjoying the calm.

"Ah fucked if I know. There's too much goin' on. I mean to say it's been a bit mental this last few days with thon priest craic an' all."

"But here, if there wasn't somethin' there'd be nothin'," said Pete.

"Aye whatever ye say Yoda," quipped back Tadhg. "Where are we anyway?"

"Well we are just into the fair county of Cork, Kanturk to be precise," answered Pete.

"Dead on, never heard of it."

"Great wee place. I came through a few years ago. Couple a good nights here but sure the local lads are all away now to Brighton or somewhere."

Tadhg turned his head away and leaned it on the door window. The vibrations gave the illusion of travelling at great speed. The snores and other winds from behind rumbled on.

"How long left?"

"'Bout two hours give or take."

"Here, can we stop for a pint or somethin'? Let them other cunts sleep."

Pete had made good progress. It was five o'clock. They'd be in Baltimore by about eight.

"Grand. Just one? Right?"

"Of course."

It was the first bar they saw. Pete pulled into the car park of The Boar's Head or An Ceann Toirc in Gaelic. It looked fairly busy judging on the number of cars.

Bit of atmosphere anyway, thought Tadhg.

Not that he minded a quiet pub, far from it. He'd played in many's a session with just the barman as audience. He enjoyed the chance of banter with strangers and new faces. He was always intrigued at the southern reaction to the crisp northern accent too. He often felt like saying 'don't be afraid, no bombs. Here check me coat'. He was scarred by the rage of it all and it was too late to change. Not too late to just roll with it though.. The north had had some serious bad press for many years. That shit sticks.

The two left the car quietly and none of the lads stirred.

"Not be long. Them hurs could smell drink a mile away," he smiled.

Decision time. It was either 'Bar' or 'Lounge'. Stools or soft seats.

"Well?" asked Pete.

"Bar. Definitely bar. My arse lost all feeling about Wicklow."

A long smooth wooden bar greeted them with waiting wooden stools and happily for Tadhg a foot rail. Not being the tallest, his legs were prone to dangle and he often had to think about where to put them. Not today. As ever, resident heads turned to see the newcomers and as quickly turned away again.

"What'll ye have lads?" asked the barmaid.

"Guinness please," answered Tadhg.

"Water for me."

"Grand so."

And off she went. She had seen several summers more than most but the manner of her greeting told Tadhg she had vast experience serving the likes of him.

"Ye friends of the deceased?" she asked still bent over so that it looked like her arse had spoken.

"Eh…no. No. We're just in for one," replied Pete.

From the bar the lounge was clearly visible. It was well populated. The air was heavy with the sorrow of someone's passing. However, there was someone singing.

Tadhg reasoned they'd been in for about five pints or so, enough to take the edge off and to let the grieving process begin. The song was long and deliberate and spoke of pain but it wasn't a tear in the beer number.

"Listen!" urged Tadhg.

It was being sung in Irish.

"It's Sliabh Geal gCua," said Pete knowingly.

Tadhg was as awake again as he'd ever been.

Who is that singing?

He stood up on the bar rail and strained to catch a glimpse of the singer but there were too many people. He sat back down and let the song drift round the room. He had heard Séamus Begley sing this one on a CD and it nearly cut the heart out of him. The lament of emigration and loss were captured in the words and air more perfectly than anything he'd ever heard.

A loud round of applause went up as did many heartfelt 'fair plays' and 'ah fuckin' lovelys'. Tadhg sat back and applauded. Pete smiled and nodded. With that Ogee led the others in.

48. Hail the Glorious Dead

"Ha, the dead arose and appeared to many," laughed Pete.

"Rip van Wankers, ye mean," added Tadhg.

"Aye ye sneaky fuckers," quipped back Ogee with a yawn.

"What's the craic?" asked McLynn. "Yiz havin' pints?"

"Aye, just to break up the journey. The snores outta ye bastards was wild," answered Tadhg. "What are ye havin'?"

Four pints of Guinness were quickly ordered and this time the bar lady kept her face forward.

"Who's dead?" asked McLynn spying the black ties and red eyes in the other room.

"How the fuck would I know?" answered Pete.

Fair point.

It was a throwaway question and a throwaway answer but it served to get them all a little closer to the action. The pints were set up like willing penguins and each took a healthy glug. From next door the strains of the whistle were heard. It was played well. Its owner had obviously listened to Vinnie Kilduff or Mary Bergin.

"Tunes," smiled O'Malaigh.

"Aye but it's the afters of a funeral or somethin'," said Tadhg.

They sat in silence for a few moments. It wasn't unheard of that a session could arise from such an occasion. They were clearly musical but these events were very family based. All sorts of feuds and grudges often emerged throughout a day's mourning. It had the potential to get awkward.

"Are ye lads musicians then?" asked the barmaid.

She knew rightly they were. Musicians have an unease in their posture when in the company of music. Fairly obvious to the trained eye of which this lady had two.

"We are indeed," answered O'Connell. "We're heading down to Baltimore for the Fiddle Fair."

"Of course. 'Tis a grand wee festival. The lad here that died was an accordion player. Played at céilís and all that. He was a fine player. Ah, 'tis a terrible thing when they're taken young," she sighed and walked away to the far side of the bar.

"Trow's down a round der Isobel," said a grey haired gentleman in a strong Cork accent. His tie was well to one side and the blazer jacket would soon be off.

"Howar'ye lads?" he said.

"Alright," said Tadhg for all.

"Were ye friends of Dónal's?" he asked.

"Ach no, we're just in for one, you know, going to the Fiddle Fair. Sorry about your loss," replied Tadhg.

"Nordern lads so. Will ye come in?"

The lads shared a quick look at each other. Pete didn't visibly object. He was intrigued by whoever had sung the song.

"Ach no, sure it's like…sure it's like a… like a funeral like," stumbled Tadhg.

"Ah not a bodder like. Ye are welcome," continued the man.

He'd clearly had a few but his generosity was genuine. The adjoining door between the bar and lounge contained an opaque square glass window with the Smithwick's Ale logo emblazoned on it.

Not too many left like that, thought Tadhg.

In they went and up to where their host stood waiting.

"Ah lads, ye are welcome. 'Twas the son that died," he explained, putting his arm around Tadhg's shoulders.

"He loved the tunes, ye know."

"Ach sorry about that," replied Tadhg a little uncomfortable at the sudden show of emotion.

In the corner the whistle started up again.

Reels.

However, the mood of the room, though content, was heavy and contained them somewhat.

"Lovely tune. Who's that playin'? asked O'Malaigh.

"That's the daughter. Kate."

"Fine stuff. Good lookin' girl too," smiled Ogee, cheekily.

"Ha! Jaysus we could have a weddin' yet," laughed the father.

"Sorry, but what's your name?" asked O'Connell.

"Connie. Connie Moloney." They clinked glasses.

He offered his hand to them all and handshakes and names were exchanged.

"Yiz are musicians so?" he asked.

"Aye," replied Tadhg.

An accordion joined in, also adeptly handled. Its owner was middle aged and he looked vacantly ahead, his mind locked into the music.

"That's Pat," said Connie, pre-empting any questions.

"Sure will ye join de lads for a tune?"

Tadhg turned and caught Pete's eye as if to say, 'Well?'

Pete nodded.

Tadhg was unsure and quickly looked to the lead musician. This was entry via the side door and he preferred to go in the front. He looked at Kate and mimed playing a fiddle. She nodded. Everyone understood.

Connie smiled.

"Ah deadly lads. Sure de boy wudda loved it like."

He turned to the room and announced them. Spaces were made next to Kate and Pat. The lads quickly retrieved their instruments and after a few more quick hellos were ready for action again.

49. The Buena Vista Céili Band

On seeing the arrival of the lads and the lifting of the mood a little, the other members of the late Dónal's céili band began to unpack their instruments. In little more than the blink of an eye the pub was a study in tuning up, handshakes and raised eyebrows at the lilting northern accent. Another round of pints was quickly administered and inevitable musical dam broken by Kate and her whistle. Tadhg and the lads waited a moment just to see what and who would follow. This crowd had undoubtedly got their own tunes and partnerships and the lads tipped gently behind all until they got a lie of the land.

The music galvanised the room. The sombre atmosphere gave way to the twist and turn of the tunes. It was as if sadness was gently being shown the door. Connie was deep in conversation at the bar but his face beamed with delight. He held the hand of, who Tadhg presumed to be, Mrs Moloney, a slight grey haired woman who had obviously cried heavily these past days. For now though she looked on and shared a smile with him. Judging on their earlier chat Tadhg felt it was just what they and their son would have wanted. There would be plenty of time for tears tomorrow and goodness knew how long after.

The session arms spread round the musicians and a bonding of sorts began. There was no need for words except for the occasional: "D'ye know dis one like?"

To which the lads nodded and joined in happily.

"Where are ye from then?" asked Kate in between breaths.

"Ach we're all sorta from Belfast," answered Pete.

"Grand. I haven't been up for ages. Is there still a session in Maddens at all?"

"Aye surely," answered Ogee. "We were just playing there yesterday or the day before. I can't remember. It's been a bit mental like with these fu…hallions, ye know."

"Indeed, I can imagine," she smiled.

She's fuckin' gorgeous, thought Tadhg.

Pete had another pint delivered to him.

This could get interesting. That's number three.

"I'm sorry about your brother. Your Da was sayin' he played the accordion."

"Jayz he did indeed. He loved the tunes; big fan of Mairtín O'Connor and Jackie Daly and all that."

"Two quare boys," said Tadhg acknowledging the two music box masters.

"Will ye lads give us a tune?" she asked.

Sufficient time had passed for this offer to be made and the lads were happy to oblige. Indeed it was the highest of compliments really.

"Ach no, yous fire on sure," answered Tadhg, adhering to the rules.

"No, go on," she insisted.

"Here, O'Connell start that one…you know thon one ye're at this years."

"Ha, fuck off," smiled O'Connell.

No sooner answered though than away he went into a reel, Mayor Harrison's Fedora no less.

"Hup, ye boy ye," shouted Kate and was straight in behind.

Tadhg now noticed more from the company drift toward their corner of the room. Whistles were produced from inside pockets and small boxes with concertinas and accordions began to emerge. In no time at all there were perhaps twenty musicians all swimming together with the current.

My first céili band.

The energy in the room moved up a notch as Dónal's team took hold of the tunes. They were obviously very well used to each other's playing and were as musically tight as a bodhrán. The lads slipped gently into their slipstream and held on. They had never really bothered with céili bands, associated as they were with competitions, pianos and snare drums. Tadhg recalled being dragged along to a real céili in Hilltown near Newry once and vowed never again. The sight of elderly women skipping about like young things frightened the life clean out of him. One lady grabbed him and pulled him into a set. It was like standing at the M2 traffic lights on a Monday morning in rush hour such was the whoosh and whirl of it all.

Whatever about the dancing the music certainly caught his ear. The band that night in Hilltown played as if they were trying to lift the building off the ground.

He felt that same power now. The Paolo Soprano accordions filled out the sound like bears. The fiddles and concertinas released their notes like racing pigeons and the whistles skipped about like honey bees. Add to this the bouzouki and bodhrán and the room was bouncing.

"Hup!" roared McLynn.

This was mighty stuff and it showed no signs of slacking off. The Paolo Soprano man moved a bit closer to Kate. She welcomed him closer still with the smile of a wife. Tadhg winked over at Ogee, who noticed it too, as if to say 'that's you blew out ye bollox.'

Ogee smiled back in acknowledgment and shrugged his shoulders in mock defeat as if to say 'well, no harm in lookin'?'

50. Perpetual Emotion

Kate remained the focus of the room. For one she was a stunner, which was enough for the lads but for two, eyes fell to her to reignite the music after each wonderful course. This task she carried out without fail for the guts of almost an hour with help here and there from accordion man. However, the baton was due to be passed along and her other half duly obliged. The Paolo Soprano box growled into life like a fine tuned Harley Davidson and in a move that threw the lads completely, he began with a set of hornpipes.

"Fuckin' hate hornpipes," whispered Ogee.

The speed of the previous tunes had loosened him right up and he was ready to really get going. Tadhg nodded in agreement. Of course he had a grudging appreciation for hornpipes and marches but in his regular session they were rare.

McLynn on the other hand let go from him a very enthusiastic 'Lovely' and was right in behind. His fiddle music came from his old teacher and fiddle maker from Ballymena, Tommy Murphy. He was well versed in such uncommon rhythms and he had garnered a wealth of such tunes. It appeared that at last he might get a chance to air them.

O'Malaigh had already put down the flute and was en route to the bar. Ogee swiftly followed. Tadhg too chose this moment to take a short break and eased himself out of the circle, leaving O'Connell supporting the tunes with his subtle chord shiftings and metronomic right arm.

"Parfil tunes, lads," said O'Malaigh. "Can't be arsed with them hornpipes though. They'll be at the marches next."

"Aye we could be here for a while," smiled Tadhg.

"There are worse places ye could be. Isobel…" shouted Ogee.

Isobel approached slowly and let a sigh out of her that briefly showed her to be a little tired.

"Same again lads?"

Before Tadhg answered he looked at Pete. He had his eyes tight closed.

"Is thon big fucker asleep?" asked Tadhg.

"Couldn't be," answered O'Malaigh. "Sure what's he had?"

As if he'd heard them he opened an eye and scanned the room. On seeing the lads at the bar he pointed to his nearly empty glass, indicating that it needed filling. He closed the eye.

"Eh, there'll be no Baltimore the night," said Ogee, laughing. "Rock n' ceol."

The pints were set up on the bar and Tadhg made for his wallet.

"No need. Der got," she said. "Connie."

"Ach fuck here, no need for that. Cheers Connie," said Tadhg and they all raised glasses in his direction.

"Get back in der now lads, 'tis early yet."

The skin behind Tadhg's ears was tightening again. He contemplated free drink, brilliant music and no idea what the fuck was going to happen next. He was happy enough with that. The lads had retaken their prized positions in the circle just as the third of the hornpipes was drawing to a close. Accordion man knew the craic. After a brief pause to let the lads get ready he slowly began again. This time his tune mirrored a roller coaster approaching the top of the ramp. He teased his way through the first half adding bass and chords where possible.

A 'Reavy' by fuck, thought Tadhg, anticipating the wondrous meanderings of the great writer's music.

And down the ramp he went with all cars full behind. The wind whooshed through the bar and the session had changed gear again. Tadhg and the lads got the heads down and followed in. Ogee let go a bark that was a mix of 'Yeehaa and hup ye bastard'. While not exactly appropriate given the circumstances no one minded in the slightest and soon echoing hoots and shouts came from the room.

Into another reel, and the intensity of the day seemed to be coming out through the accordion keys themselves. The selection of minor tunes, mixolydian tunes with naturals all over the place, almost blues like, dragged up deep emotions.

Tadhg wondered how the set would end, not that he wanted it to. His fingers danced merrily up and down the neck of his fiddle, each string getting plenty of attention. There was 'other' going on, an extra element in the room. Pete's eyes were wide open and staring hard at some object on the wall. The music had him, he was 'away'. He tapped his whole leg and Tadhg waited for a red Superman-like laser beam to shoot from his eyes. The second half of the latest tune now beckoned and the company knew this set was drawing to a close. Tadhg readied himself and caught the eye of accordion man who in turn quickly glanced around at as many as he could. With a long draw on the last note, basses blaring he brought things to a halt and smiled widely. Job done.

Pete stood and let a loud 'parfil' out of him and slowly sat again. He had found the singer from earlier and they were talking about songs. Ogee laughed out loud and narrowly avoided spraying stout from his gob. O'Malaigh put his flute down and in the same motion grabbed hold of his pint as if he'd just run a marathon. It sloshed over the glass and round his lips. O'Connell timed his strum to perfection, dead stop. Bang. He also made for the black. McLynn moved his bow to his fiddle hand so that he held both there and reached for his pint. Tadhg did likewise and acknowledged accordion man with a respectful glance and nod. It said all that needed saying. The remainder of the circle collectively inhaled and let the wave pass over them. The room yelled their approval as loud as their hearts allowed, caught as they were between sorrow and its release.

51. The Rare Oul' Times

Eugene's last sojourn through the great city of Dublin was at a time when the road leaned and dipped through the smaller towns and villages of Dundalk, Dunleer and the like. He now found himself on the M50 or as he liked to refer to it 'the Monstrous 50'.

European money, he thought. *Where would we have been without it? Probably a damn site better off now that we have to pay it back.*

It saddened him greatly to see his beloved Ireland in such a calamitous state. He felt the country had become a stranger to him.

Bloody Celtic Tiger. I'd skin the damn thing.

He had stopped watching RTE altogether and enjoyed TG4 a lot more.

RTE, CNN, BBC…the same oul crap!

He recalled a time when news was informative or at least that's how it felt. The news broadcasters looked and sounded like normal people for the most part. There was some comfort to be found in the undramatic news title music and the monotonous delivery. They were telling him something then. Now he found it hard to distinguish any of the news channels or brands. All dolled up, music, graphics, short skirts and banality. He didn't care for news readers having personalities.

Then the Tiger hit and Ireland became America and Britain and Europe over night.

Sure what did we know about money? We were poor for most of our lives. Like a child in a bloody sweet shop we were but by God we're paying dear now.

His thoughts skimmed around his brain ruffling feathers of feelings that the music would subsequently calm. His head was often full of such inner conversations so much so that when driving he would occasionally forget certain parts of the journey. As it was he was through the worst of new Dublin and heading south. The Naas dual carriageway now appeared to him as wide as the Nile and full of crocodiles. It rolled into the distance. He rolled with it glancing at the occasional filling stations alongside and tutting at the price of fuel. The new-monied roads began to gently ebb away and the remnants of an earlier more thinly tarred Ireland seeped under his wheels.

The car shuddered over a pothole, then another and then about five in a row. He felt it all the way down to his behind. Not a good vibration. Not for the car anyhow. Eugene took a little comfort in it.

They haven't got us all yet then.

His arse was now part of the revolution.

A hiker by God.

Sure enough in the distance he saw the unmistakeable shape of someone gearing up to put the thumb out. Evidently this one was in the early stages of the lift hunt. Shoulders unslumped, thumb out at ninety degrees and the dead giveaway itself…a smile. By his side a guitar case. Eugene had seen many barely fit to raise their hands and had often got the fingers in the rear view mirror as he drove passed. This one would be getting a lift.

"Ah cheers mate, thanks very much," said the passenger, as he sat himself into the front seat, guitar placed along the back.

"Where are ye far?" asked Eugene, giving the gear stick a shake to make sure of its neutrality.

"Ah I'm heading down to Baltimore actually. The Fiddle Fair, you heard of it?"

"Baltimore? Ha! I'm heading that way myself. Guitar player then?"

"Aye, for my sins."

I could help you there.

"I know it's the Fiddle Fair but I don't think they'll mind too much," said the passenger in hope.

"No I'm sure not," replied Eugene.

As long as you play it half bloody decent.

"My name's Jimi, by the way."

Good name.

"I'm Eugene. Have ye heard this boy before?"

Eugene hit play on the cd player and Maguire once again filled the air.

"Maguire?" asked Jimi.

"The very same."

"Aye sure I met him once and he started playing me guitar."

Sounds about right.

"No offence Eugene but he was no guitar player. Total genius though on the fiddle."

"Ye ever heard him on the pipes?" asked Eugene, trying to place his passenger's accent.

Jimi laughed aloud.

"The pipes? No, what was he like?"

"He was a genius on the fiddle," replied Eugene and left it there.

"So where are you from?"

"Melbourne."

"You're far from home by God," said Eugene half shocked.

"Oh I don't know. I'm half Irish as they say. Mum was from Newry. We moved back a good few years ago. I suppose I have a bit of a twang still."

"Aye, not much to be fair. You'll have heard of Cooney then?"

"Steve? Yea surely mate, he's a friend of the father's. Oul' session buddies they were. I'm hoping to meet up with him actually. I heard he's playing with Martin Hayes at the Fair."

"What a team," said Eugene.

52. Lights out, lights on

Tadhg became aware of being cold first. He then became aware of his cheek being against a type of soft plastic. His eyes were still closed and his brain flickered like the lights in a huge factory first thing in the morning. He then realised that he was in a seat of some kind as his back was up against a similar type of soft cushion or something. He was then able to stretch a little but not too far. His feet, boots still on, hit against an obstacle.

What the fuck?

On opening his eyes he found himself in the back seat of a car.

Peugeot.

As to who's car? Where? How? He had no idea. His confusion and no little panic was lifted however when in the rear view mirror he saw Pete and the rest of them standing beside Pete's car changing a wheel.

What? Car park? Cork, funeral, tunes, whiskies. Peugeot!

The car itself was not in great shape. The carpets were holed and dust ridden. The front seats had been covered in an old seat cover from the seventies and there were sweet and crisp wrappers and empty chip trays scattered in the back and front. He sat up and looked around. The light in the sky told him it was still fairly early, perhaps ten-ish maybe eleven. He clambered out.

Where's the fiddle?

The lads at the wheel on seeing their comrade let go the usual barrage of cheers, jeers and 'state a thats'.

Tadhg walked over unsteadily to join them.

"Alright," he said.

What he meant was 'how did I end up there?'

"Well ye rocket? Quer fuckin' head on ye the day," laughed Ogee.

"Jesus. But? How in the name of fuck?" asked Tadhg, not really wanting the answer. "Did someone buy whiskey? O'Malaigh ye cunt, did you buy them French frogs again?"

"Laphroaig you mean? They're Scottish ye twat," laughed O'Malaigh. "Course, we couldn't carry them to ye!"

"Oh Jesus, aye. Christ the night. What about the wake an' all? Where did ye end up?" asked Tadhg, now at a complete loss.

"Ach things began to wind up shortly after Pete's song," began O'Connell.

He sang?

"Fuck me, mate. I don't mind that at all," mumbled a guilty Tadhg.

"Aye well the father, yer man, what ye call him?

"Connie," said Tadhg.

"Aye Connie. He kinda had enough all of a sudden too. Himself and the wife bade us goodnight and headed on."

"He shook your hand Tadhg and got you the first of the whiskies," continued O'Connell.

Vague memories.

Walked outside...stars...Orion's belt...

"He then said that the daughter, the good looking one, was staying with them that night and asked her to put us all up. So we ended up in her kitchen just up the road, staggering distance, with the husband playing tunes and drinkin' 'til the wee small hours."

"And why the fuck didn't ye take me?" asked Tadhg in faux outrage.

"Sure we couldn't find ye, ye bin lid? We checked the loo and the ladies loo. No sign."

"We checked under the pool table, in the beer store, the fuckin' kitchen but no sign and sure we were all fuckin' steamboats ourselves," added Ogee.

Car door was open, thought Tadhg.

Pete then brought a little momentum to proceedings.

"I saw ye flat out in the back seat and there was no movin' ye. But we're here now. We getting this wheel changed or what?"

The lads helped in whatever way they could which was mostly to stand and look at Pete change the wheel. Tadhg stood with his thoughts.

"Fuck, where's the fiddle?" he asked.

"All instruments accounted for ye plank," said McLynn. "I put yours away last night for all the fuck you gave about it."

"Cheers," replied Tadhg.

Cure.

He looked at his watch, then at Ogee who telepathically knew it was about one minute to opening time.

"Scene of the crime and all that…" said O'Malaigh, catching the scent on the wind.

"Aye, just the one," laughed Pete.

The wheel was tightened, the jack replaced just as Isobel bade them a good morning from the door of the pub.

"Mornin' lads," she smiled. "Ye were in fine tune last night."

Tadhg went over and gave her a hug.

"Jesus, Isobel, ye near killed me."

"Ha, if you can't shtand de heat don't drink bloody whiskey so," she laughed.

"Can we get married?" asked Tadhg.

"Ah go on wit' yerself," she replied and headed inside smiling.

"Five pints and a coffee," said Pete.

The taste of Guinness is medicine and ailment all in one at times. Tadhg felt the coldness of it but knew a revival wasn't too far away.

53. Come West along the Road

An hour or so later the lads were well and truly drawing in on Baltimore itself. The towns leading to it whistled by the car windows not that many saw them. Sleep and fatigue had taken them for the time being. Pete was glad this final leg was only a small hop compared to the previous ones. He did wonder at the proud distinction west Cork natives used. They weren't from Cork but west Cork and damned be the one that forgot it.

Bit like Antrim and north Antrim, he mused.

Millstreet, Doneraile and Macroom were safely negotiated to snores and farts and 'ah by the holy fucks'. The escape and stench of wind forced him to open the window on several occasions. The cool air did refresh him though and he took a moment to consider just where and why he was here. Having lived in Belfast most of his adult life he had been deeply scarred by the politics and violence of it all. It was fairly inevitable that he became involved in the fightback as he saw it. However, he restricted his activities to street protests and murals and that type of thing. As well as Dire Straits, he always loved singing and had become a regular at the local session haunts in Belfast. His sheer size did go against him and he was at times a target for drunken in-fighting between the various shades of republicanism in the city. It tightened him up though and he was more than a match for any half assed assault that came his way.

He became intrigued with Tadhg's story on hearing it from his father who was a second cousin of Tadhg's mum (or was it a third cousin?) Anyway, here he was steering history for the better. Dunmanway appeared on a sign.

Not far now, he thought.

Roadside red fuchsias grew in amazing number here. He stopped briefly and grabbed a handful. Their aroma off-set the perma-fart fog of the back seat. They reminded him too of a wee weekend away he had with an old flame many moons ago. He found now that he preferred the single life but of course would pull the knickers off a quare one should the opportunity arise. He felt very much at ease down among the hedges of west Cork. These roads were soft highways to craic, music and general divilment. They seemed to invite mischief and he was happy to oblige. Of course he regretted the occasional incident like the show at wee Tom's but really that was not all that common an occurrence. He felt he shared that sense of 'letting go the world' with Tadhg and had enjoyed his company these last few days.

Drimoleague.

Half an hour'll do it.

"Where are we?" asked Tadhg.

The fast air of the open window had awoken him.

"About half an hour away."

"Ah great. How ye getting' on?"

"Aye, grand. You?"

"Recovering. By the way, Pete, thanks for this you know."

"Fuck up," came the tart response. Pete wasn't one for the mutual back slap.

Tadhg took the point and smiled. Pete had said 'you're quite welcome' in his own way.

Then came an unexpected voice,

"Oh father dear, the day will come when vengeance loud will call
And we'll arise with Erin's boys and rally one and all
I'll be the man to lead the van, beneath our flag of green
And loud and high we'll raise the cry, "Revenge for Skibbereen!"

The others sat and listened intently as O'Malaigh sang in operatic fervour, albeit a little croakily, the final verse of that great Irish song of loss and rebellion. As he Pavorotti'd the last line the whole car joined in. Tadhg wondered if ever a sign on a road got such a musical greeting. The song had stirred their souls and ignited their spirits after sleep. Lethargy was booted out of the window and anticipation rushed in. It's not that often people from one end of the country make it to the other and of them all only O'Malaigh had been down more than once.

"Ah Skibb," he sighed. "How I've missed your creamy pints."

But there would no stopping in Skibbereen today. Pete kept the hammer down and after another twenty minutes the end of the rainbow itself, Baltimore appeared before them.

54. Mick the Flick

Eugene had bid farewell to Jimi the previous evening with promise of reunion and spent a very agreeable night in a local B&B. His stomach was forcing its way out through the buttons of his shirt such was the generosity of the breakfast. West Cork is famous for many things and one of those is black pudding or spiced pig's blood. It was not a common taste for Eugene. Marry that with eggs, sausages, bacon, mushrooms and beans and toast and it was unsurprising that Eugene felt he'd never have to eat again.

He left the beautifully comfy room and ventured out into Baltimore itself. It reminded him no end of Ballycastle with the sound and smell of the sea on the air. However, it had its own layout and there were a myriad of corners, wee streets and alleyways to remember. He remarked on the amount of visitors mulling around and just how many were carrying fiddle cases.

Fiddle Fair, he thought. *Fantastic. Might listen to a few tunes…*

He walked slowly through the streets and ended up at the front of a bar with surely one the finest views in Ireland, looking out as it did over the Atlantic. Its front was a meeting place for foot and tyre as the main road passed by but there was more than adequate room for pedestrians, tables and potential to sit and look around. He heard the unmistakable strains of bow on string coming from within. He checked his watch. .

One twenty. Early start.

He walked in to the large bar and admired the long, curved wooden serving area replete with beer and Guinness taps and the usual line up of spirits standing to attention behind. The glasses were sparkling beneath in their little stacks four and five high. He followed his ears. They led him to a corner on the right wherein sat a lone fiddler just going over a couple of loosener jigs to get the arm going. Familiar or not the jigs were played with great feel and touch. Eugene watched the bow dance over the strings and knew the owner of that arm had been long in the saddle. Then without warning the bow shot straight off the high E string into the air and back down again without missing a note.

Mick the Flick? Could it be him?

A second flick a moment later confirmed his suspicions. The first fiddle he heard and it was none other than 'the Flick' himself. Eugene turned back toward the bar and ordered a coffee. How would he play this?

I should let Tadhg find him, shouldn't I?
What? That lad could hardly find his bloody fingers at the end of his arm.
No, that's not fair. Say nothing, just say hello and see what happens…

Mick scanned the room from time to time mid tune and for the briefest of moments the two men made eye contact. Eugene nodded to signal how much he was enjoying the tune and sat just a few tables away. Mick returned to the business at hand.

To look at Mick then with his delicacy amongst the notes would be to see an image of Ireland as is and as the world would expect. His hair, what remained of it, was scattered without purpose across the top of his head. It was a grey/silver and hinted in places at being brown at one time. His face was the stuff of old boat bows, oak trees and statues. The lines on his forehead were deep carved especially now with the concentration required to play. His eyebrows were full and still the brown colour of his youth. Eugene noticed his fingers next. They were all knuckles and skin, long and thin too. They had not seen bricks or mortar much but were not the protected fingers of an office clerk either. Mick's flat cap sat beside him on the seat.

His selection of tunes finished and Eugene offered a respectful applause, just a couple of claps with a 'lovely' on the end. "Ah good man, tenks," said Mick.

The west Cork accent is of the sea and sounds like water, wit, wisdom and 'watch out' are sewn into every word. Eugene was about to reply when several other musicians appeared as if by magic behind him and joined Mick. They prepared themselves and the opportunity to chat was gone. Eugene sipped his coffee and decided to just relax and enjoy the music.

Mick's three companions were not in the first flush of youth by any means nor were they falling apart at the seams. Eugene guessed that he and they were perhaps of an age. They gathered with two extra fiddles and a flute.

Fierce traditional.

After the requisite tapping of strings and twisting of flute they began without a word into a lovely set of reels. Eugene watched them and the unity of the bows matched by the slow dancing shoulders of the flautist.

Such grace, borne from a lifetime's practice and a long time in each other's company.

And there it was again…the flick. The bow up off the strings like a bird off a branch and back as quick. Eugene listened to the tunes and they took him away to his youth. Days of practicing for fleadhs and céili bands, camaraderie and craic. A coffee or two later the session paused to look around and the music stopped for a moment. Two of the musicians headed to the bar leaving Mick and one other to hold the seat, not that anyone would have dreamed of sitting there. This would be the moment to say hello and he approached reverently. Mick saw him and smiled, stood up and offered his hand.

"Howrye Eugene, it's been a long time."

55. The Music House

Tadhg trembled, breathed deeply and ran his fingers through his hair. Whether it was the drink dying in him or the realization that they had at last reached their destination he wasn't sure. What he did know was he had to find some old fiddler and with any luck get his hands on a right few quid. But there was more to it. His mother had walked these narrow streets in which he now found himself, as had he as a child. Pete had slowed the car to walking pace to negotiate the curves and crannies that pretended to be streets. Tadhg loved towns like this, where the roof tops were almost on his shoulders. He felt he could clear a crow's nest out of a chimney pot with a good run and jump.

Being all new to the town no one really had any advice to give Pete other than remark on each bar or chip shop that they noticed. After a few moments they found themselves at the end of the road looking into the sea. There was a fleet of small boats moored on ropes and a pier that stretched some hundred yards toward America.

"What? Is that it?" asked Ogee.

"We miss a turn or something?" groaned McLynn.

"Tits on yer one!" was O'Malaigh's contribution.

"Jaysus, they're all out the day," said O'Connell, remarking on the hive of Scandinavian looking girls walking toward them.

"Christ the night," gasped Ogee. "I love it already."

"Right Tadhg, you're the captain. What's the story?"

"Pint."

Pete smiled. He'd taken the word right out of his mouth. No driving for the foreseeable.

"No harm to anyone but I need a fuckin' bed tonight," said O'Malaigh.

"Aye and deloused," added Ogee.

"Listen to him," snapped back O'Malaigh. "Jesus, you're fuckin' hummin'."

"Aye, so's yer Ma," quipped back Ogee.

The banter continued thus until Pete parked near the pier. They got out and looked around and inhaled deeply the fresh sea air. Other than Ballycastle, the lads really didn't get to the seaside very often. Their lungs were pleasantly surprised.

"Right wankers, B&B time," said Pete, the pint thought quickly overcome.

He marched resolutely up the gentle incline to the front of a pub. The light of day shone on their pallid faces and they looked like the remnants of a vampire stag night.

"Class, isn't it?" said Tadhg, looking around again.

He was as far from home as he could be on the island of Ireland. He felt remote but not alone. He had his mates about him and there was a lot to be said for it. That and the fact that everyone seemed to be carrying, or in close proximity to someone carrying a fiddle.

Holy God. 'Tis like Al Capone's wedding.

At the top of the incline the letters spelling 'McCarthy's Bar' were unmissable, especially to this crack unit of drink commandos.

"Tadhg, I'm gonna find a B&B, ye comin'?" asked Pete.

There was no great protest from the lads this time. There was need of a small break from the gargle and they all knew it.

"Aye, c'mon sure. We'll come back down in a while," answered Tadhg.

They didn't have far to go as protruding from the side of a gable wall they saw another sign 'Teach an Cheoil B&B'.

The Music House. Fate? wondered Tadhg.

"Here, we'll be lucky to get somewhere I'd say," said O'Malaigh. "With the Fair an' all."

No one replied and Tadhg knocked the door. His first impression was that the small house would hardly be fit to hold a cat never mind six ripe and weary travellers. A shadow moved behind the glass front door.

"Hello, howrye? Any rooms there at all?"

The young lad behind the door was all of about sixteen.

"How many like?" he asked, his accent raising in pitch toward the end of the question.

"Ach two'd be great," answered Tadhg not feeling hopeful.

"Hold on a minute…Mum! Mum!"

A moment later 'mum' joined him. He slipped off quietly behind her. She was a slight woman, thin with short brown hair that had been occasionally fussed over by a hairdresser. She had a landlady's face on her and could read people.

"Ken I help ye lads?"

"Aye we're lookin' two rooms," asked Tadhg again.

"Ah now leds, ye are leevin' it fierce late. Sure the Fiddle Fair is on like, ye know?"

"Aye, I see that but we saw your sign agus tá giota Gaeilge agam (I have a little Irish) and just thought we'd ask, ye know."

"Uh huh. Where are ye from so?"

"Ach up near Belfast mostly but we came from Ballycastle a few days ago… though it seems like a week now."

"D'old Lemmis Fair. Ha, I was there once. Lovely place. And ye came all the way here for the music?" she asked, intrigued.

"Aye, we did," answered Tadhg. "Sure we're not wise."

The others looked as harmless and friendly as they could which despite their dishevelled appearance was no great difficulty. They were, deep down, quite harmless and very friendly.

"Well your luck is in leds. We had a crowd der from America booked in but dey cancelled just an hour ago. C'mon in so."

"Ah, God bless America," sang O'Malaigh and in they went.

56. In the Flickering Light

The lads split into both rooms, Pete, Tadhg and Ogee in one and O'Connell, McLynn and O'Malaigh in the other. Each room had a double bed and a single which brought about the usual bartering and hurried dumping of bags on the single bed. Each that had to share secretly hoped their partner did not piss the bed or lay eggs. After each had had a quick wash they were ready to head back into town. It was late afternoon.

"Here, we'll try that McCarthy's. Looked a good spot," offered O'Malaigh.

"Aye, I'm starvin'. Steak n chips comin' up," answered Ogee.

Deal done. Without further word they headed back toward McCarthy's. It wasn't long before they heard the sounds of fiddles and flute.

"Tunes," smiled McLynn.

The lads headed in and their in-built 'suss out' gene kicked in. Each surveyed every inch they could see. This survival instinct was a reminder of a dark time in northern history and they did it automatically. Soon enough shoulders loosened and they remembered they were far from Belfast and steel shadows.

"Well fuck me. Look who it is," said Pete, looking in the direction of an elderly gentleman with eyes closed, lost in the music.

"Brilliant," laughed Ogee.

"Here, Tadhg, you might as well wake him up," said O'Connell.

Tadhg saw him too; father, stranger, priest and part of the adventure.

"Ye made it ye boy ye. Fair play," said Tadhg from just behind Eugene's left shoulder.

Eugene swung around to see the troupe and hear a chorus of 'well Father's, 'bout ye's' and the like.

"Tadhg! Good man. Sit down, sit down. Lads come over, come on," offered Eugene.

Pete headed to the bar and the first order of the afternoon was duly made. Whether by instinct or other the lads didn't take their places at the table but instead followed Pete up to the bar. They guessed that there was something to be discussed by Tadhg, the priest and Pete in much the same way as they had in wee Tom's.

"Ach yer grand Father. We'll get a pint and be down in a minute sure," said McLynn.

"Ok well, ok," replied Eugene.

He cut straight to it.

"Tadhg, do you see that man there on the right playing the fiddle?"

"Aye."

"That is 'Mick the Flick'."

Tadhg scanned the old boy.

Fuck, he'd be about eight stone soaking wet. Head on him like a hairy egg and wiry too.

"You sure?"

"Tadhg, you wouldn't believe it but he only stood up and shook my hand when I met him and said 'howrye Eugene'!"

"You know him?"

"Well I didn't remember at first but it seems I do, although don't really."

"Aye, that sounds good."

"What I mean is he knew your mum very well even when I was…well, we were…you know, stepping out."

Shaggin' ye mean.

"Go on…"

"Well all those years ago your mum and me headed where the music was, particularly that summer. Of course she had been doing this long before I was on the scene. Nevertheless we went together to wee festivals like Drumshanbo and Tobercurry and even up to Teelin in Donegal. You know the craic, there are certain people you just meet at festivals. Perhaps for three days a year for maybe 20 years or at least until the festival dies or you or your friends do."

"Aye, I'm with you."

At that moment Pete sat down with three pints and a packet of Tayto.

"They're not the same you know," he said as he opened the packet.

"Cheers…what's not?" asked Eugene.

"These oul' Mexican crisps. Same name right enough although how can that be with copyright an' all I don't know. But they taste like shite."

"Didn't stop ye buyin' them ye bollocks," replied Tadhg. "Here, enough about crisps. Ye might as well hear this."

"Ok, well," began Eugene again. "Turns out that Mick and your mum were festival friends. They always ended up in the same camp site, circle or session or pub or party or whatever."

"Aye, that happens alright," said Pete.

"So did he see you with mum?"

"He did. Now to be honest I had eyes only for your mum and I sort of kidnapped her a bit if you know what I mean. Time was short and I just wanted to be with her, you know."

"So he remembered you from the sessions?" asked Pete.

"He did indeed. Memory like a pool player," said Tadhg, referring to his occasional past time and recalling every frame he'd ever lost.

"Whenever I left the scene, not knowing about you, you understand, Mick kinda took your mum under his wing and she lived down here."

"Like… with him?" asked Tadhg.

"Yes but not *with* him, you know," said Eugene. "Just good friends."

"Fuck," said Tadhg and looked at Mick again. He had just gone up enormously in his opinion.

"And he has the answers to mum's riddle?"

"Well you're not gonna find out askin' us ye plank," said Pete.

This was it. Tadhg just looked again at the old man who had treated his mother so kindly.

Christ, what do I say?

57. Inner Workings

Tadhg waited. He just couldn't land in in the middle of the tunes. He would wait and observe the unwritten rules handed down from session player to session player over hundreds of years. He listened carefully to the musicians and knew that they were in the second half of the tune. The end of the set was approaching. They finished as one and Mick flicked the bow just ever so slightly higher than normal. He had noticed Tadhg talking to Eugene and wondered who the man tank was sitting beside them. Tadhg's fears as to how he would approach Mick were unfounded as Mick stood up and walked toward their table.

Tadhg's stomach tightened and he felt queasy and anxious.

"Howrye leds? Would you be Tadhg by any chance?" he asked and offered his hand.

Tadhg shook it warmly.

"I am indeed. Would you be Mick the Flick? And where's the fiddle? I saw ye were sellin' one," replied Tadhg quickly with a grin.

"Ha, I am. But it has just gone off the market, 'tis yours. Your mum gave it to me but after waitin' for ye for years I decided just recently I'd sell it. Needn't a bothered. She nick-named me that for obvious reasons," he smiled widely.

He seemed delighted to meet them.

"Ha, good job I got it in time."

Fate?

"This is all a bit mad Mick," began Tadhg. "You knew mum well, this man is my father which I only found out on Sunday and Pete here is the deliverer of letters and life changing news."

"Happy to help," smiled Pete.

"Yes that sounds a bit different Tadhg but your mum was really the most wonderful woman. She went about things in her own way. Of course you heard ye were born just under that table."

"Yes, different eh?"

Mick pulled up his chair so that he was opposite Tadhg. He took a drink of his pint and shouted over to the other musicians that this was the session baby from all those years ago. They looked at Tadhg, waved and smiled as if to say 'turned out alright' or 'turned out like a feckin' ejit'. It was hard to know. They turned back into their seats and into a set of hornpipes.

"I think she found the normal road boring because she didn't exactly make it easy for herself. But, sayin' that she enjoyed life and my goodness was she proud of you."

"Yes we got on pretty well. So I lived here for a few years. Can't say I remember much about it, sorry. She didn't talk about Baltimore."

"No, sure ye were only small. Yer mam took you up to Newry then. Itchy feet I think and a bit closer to family. You would only have been two or three. We missed her but I saw her from time to time at festivals. She stopped coming, I suppose as you grew up and started school and all, and we drifted apart. I'd get an odd postcard with pictures of Newry Canal and the Town Hall now and again. Good fun, you know."

"Aye, that sounds like her," replied Tadhg, realising his effect on her life.

"Now, before she left we had a fantastic session at that same table we're at tonight. You were there in a little carry cot," said Mick pointing to the corner nearest the musicians' table.

"Great tunes I'm sure," said Eugene.

"Well at the end of it she and me were standing out at the front there looking into the night and talking, you know the way you do, and both of us quite tipsy of course. So suddenly like she gives me a big hug outta de blue and says 'will ye take care of this for me?' Sure I near shit the pants. Didn't I think she was talking about you!"

"Ha," laughed Tadhg.

"No she wasn't for givin' ye away. She meant the fiddle. Actually, that fiddle. Over there."

Mick pointed to the fiddle he'd been playing so well. It sat up proudly against the upholstered seat and seemed to survey to whole bar. The bow stood guard like alongside. He got up and lifted it and placed it on the table in front of them.

Tadhg looked at it. It felt for a moment his mother had reincarnated into this musical instrument.

"Now, I know," began Mick again. "'Tis far from the best fiddle in the world. In fact 'tis fair rough around the edges. But it plays beautifully. There's something going on with it I can't explain."

Tadhg thought of the Ballymena fiddle maker who could explain every inch of it to him.

"Your mam always said it was magic."

"Ach here, now," laughed Pete. "Magic fiddle my hole. What is this? Darby O'fuckin' Gill! No disrespect or anythin' like."

"None taken," replied Mick. "I'm pretty sure she meant the sound of it, you know. It shouldn't be that good but just somehow is."

Tadhg smiled again. She always told him stories about magic and fairies and music. He carried them deep within him still.

"Yes, that'd be her."

He picked up the fiddle by the neck as if a piece of bone china. He placed it under his chin and picked up the bow. He felt like he was giving her a hug.

He ushered out of it a few notes and as quickly put it down.

"Lovely indeed."

From his inside pocket Tadhg removed the letter Pete had given him and showed it to Mick. He read it quickly, nodding slowly as he did so.

"So, do you know what she is on about? What clue is she talking about?" asked Tadhg.

"Christ," gasped Mick. "£15,000!"

He took another swig of his pint.

"The only thing she ever gave me was this fiddle. There must be something in it."

"But what could you put in a fiddle?" asked Eugene.

"And how would you ever find it without wreckin' it?" asked Pete.

"If I'm not mistaken there's one thing in there that ye could maybe put something in…the sound post. And if ye have the right tool ye can remove it without too much damage."

"The what?" asked Pete.

"The sound post ye balloon," replied Tadhg. "It's a wee circular wooden dowel that supports the interior of the fiddle and transfers the sound around it. It's only a few centimeters long and just a bit fatter than a healthy nail."

Tadhg lifted the fiddle up to the light and could see it inside.

"And there she is. We have to get it out," he said. "Right now."

58. Curiouser and curious hurs

The lads at the bar had supped the first deliriously frothy sups of their Guinness and had noticed Tadhg lift the fiddle above his head.

"What the fuck's he at?" asked O'Malaigh.

"Dunno. Looking for something," answered Ogee.

"In a fiddle?" asked O'Connell. "Never seen that before."

"Hmmm, I might know," said McLynn.

He was something of a fiddle nut and although he never made one he had on occasion been to workshops and was enthralled at the process from block of wood to instrument of kings and working men in equal measure. He led them over to the table.

"What ye at, Tadhg?" he asked.

Tadhg held the fiddle up, twisting it this way and that.

"Good question. I've just inherited this and well it's a long story lads but I think there might be something pretty valuable in 'er. I just need something to get that sound post out."

"Right," said O'Connell, a little sarcastically.

"Shit, I know the yoke too but I don't have one," said McLynn. "But there is something that'd do it…"

"Aye, go on," said Tadhg.

"I need a bra," said McLynn.

"Here have mine," laughed Pete.

"No, serious. Ye can twist the wire in them to hook it out."

Ogee's eyes visibly brightened.

"How long have we got?" he asked, rising to the challenge.

"No panic like, but the sooner the better," said Tadhg. "But sure there must be a wee hardware shop in town, Mick?"

"Aye but 'tis closed on a Winsday like."

"Shit. Right. Well, bra wire it is. Anybody pulls that off and it's free pints for a month."

As if they needed any encouragement to disrobe young ladies, the lads clinked glasses to seal the deal.

"Do you mind if we join ye for a tune Mick," asked Tadhg.

"Ah Jesus, we'd be delighted. Can I use this in the meantime?" he replied smiling widely, pointing at the fiddle. "I'll tell the lads to make a space."

"Of course, as long as ye give it back after," laughed Tadhg.

Mick left the table and headed back with the fiddle. He squeezed himself into his place and Tadhg noticed him tell the others to expect company. The men looked around again to offer entrance. Their hair had been ravaged to varying degree by time and hinted of grey and lack of combs.

"Tunes lads?" asked Tadhg.

There was nothing else for it for the time being.

"Aye why not?" said O'Connell.

They stood up and headed out of the bar down to the car. It was now late evening and the sun was preparing to clock off for the day. Their shadows stretched before them as they approached the sea front again. They removed their instruments from the boot and returned ready for action once again.

"I feel a second wind comin' on," said O'Connell. The session potential proved catalyst to energy. Even though tiredness was hinting at rest and a quiet moment, the sheer enjoyment and power of traditional music was swaying the argument its way.

"What's the long story then Tadhg?" asked McLynn. "I kinda guessed there was a bit more to it than the Fiddle Fair."

"It wouldn't take a genius would it?" added Ogee. "What's the craic, dude?"

Tadhg took a few steps closer to the bar then turned to face them.

"Lads, what can I tell ye? Turns out the priest is my Da, I lived here for nearly three years, Mick took care of me and there's fifteen grand in thon fiddle."

Stunned silence.

"Ah fuck away off," laughed O'Connell. "I believe ye, thousands wouldn't."

"Ha, perfect," said McLynn.

"Sweet to the beat," smiled Ogee.

That was it. They just looked at him and smiled. Tadhg knew that whatever he told them they'd stick it out with him, so might as well tell the truth. If you have one good friend in life you're lucky, Tadhg had a handful and he felt ready for anything.

59. The Lovely Girls

The gold at the end of the fiddle bow had the similar effect as that of walking with a small stone in your shoe. No matter how much he played Tadhg could not get the little sound post out of his mind. The potential to finish the adventure was proving overwhelming and stirred in him some painful thoughts. He would far rather have been able to make this journey with his mum or least see her after all. She would have loved every minute of it.

He was a session-child thanks to her and not a day went by that he wasn't thankful for it. His first live music was heard from underneath a table dodging tapping feet and drops of Guinness from above. From there it was music lessons and just picking up whatever instrument was at hand in the house. He met his mother's friends who were invariably ridiculously talented, warm hearted near geniuses and learned the 'trad' way. In Newry there were kitchen sessions and parties where the music was as good as any headline act at any festival. From there to fleadhs, festivals and friends on every part of the island. He was one of the many bearers of Ireland's very heartbeat. As that moment however he bore the bursting need for a piss.

Tadhg excused himself from the session which was still in first gear. On his return from the toilet he decided to take a step outside, just for a breath.

Again he was mesmerised by the view and the whole bloody escapade. The music called him back. He heard it seep out between the pores in the concrete, through the putty in the windows and he wasn't going to refuse. He glanced toward the car and noticed one pull in alongside Pete's. Curiosity held him there a moment. The long legs held him a moment longer. He recognised that arse.

Well fuck me.

From the car spilled the girls from In Nomine Patri et Fili. They each had a bottle of something.

Smirnoff…WKD…cider. Ha! Brilliant.

He watched on as they giggled and sorted themselves the way girls do. Tadhg just saw shorts and pressured tops. He sighed happily at the view.

Up the hill they came toward the pub carrying their various weapons of mass entertainment.

"Will ye look at the state a that?" he shouted.

They laughed and yahoo'd in reply like it was going out of business.

"Tadhg! Ye made it," said Rosie.

He noticed her flute and thought (and hoped) her smile was a little more enthusiastic than for just civility.

"Of course, sure we're playin' tunes. Yiz comin' in?"

"Don't ye know we are?" she replied. "We'll just leave the bags into the B&B. We're booked into a wee place somewhere. Maura has it all sorted. Did ye get a place?"

"Aye, just left it. We had it booked ages ago ye know. Didn't wanna risk not gettin' somewhere."

"Yer arse," retorted Rosie laughing

Jesus, she knows me already.

"Ha, aye no, we were dead lucky, just got in on a cancellation about an hour ago."

"Fair play. Right where's the tunes at?" she asked.

"Up there. McCarthy's. Tune central by the looks of things," he answered.

The other girls approached giggling and in great form.

"Well Tadhg," said Sarah, the red head. "How are you?"

"Great. Sure c'mon. Get your instruments and we'll have a tune. I can think of a few lads be delighted to see yiz."

The four girls walked up the small incline leaving Maura to make the necessary B&B arrangements. She headed up past the pub. She gave her accordion box to Cassie who now held both that and her own smaller concertina box.

"See ye shortly," she said as she juggled four small bags over her shoulders.

"Yiz are travelling light…you know…" began Tadhg.

"For girls?" finished Sorcha, swapping her banjo from hand to hand.

"Aye…well, you know normally it's a suitcase per half day away like," said Tadhg smiling.

"Yea well, we're here for the craic. We'll get dressed up at the wedding," replied Sorcha, pinching Rosie.

Tadhg felt himself blush a bit.

Jesus, am I that obvious?

There were now an orchestra of thoughts running through Tadhg's mind. From Rosie's loveliness, to uses for her bra, to revealing the secret of the fiddle, to the ensuing carnage of what was now shaping up to be the daddy of all sessions. He hung back a moment and let the others go into McCarthy's.

Ah fuck it.

"Here Rosie?"

"Follow yiz in… Aye?" she asked, all smiles.

"Any chance you'd take your bra off?"

60. The Beacon

"Sure here's my knickers too," she snapped and turned away.

She was completely deflated with a look that asked 'are you just another wanker?'

"No, hold on Rosie. It's not like that at all."

Well it is a bit.

Tadhg quickly explained his situation and Rosie slowly turned from someone about to donate a fist to his nose to a keen and intrigued listener. Tadhg was mightily relieved to see her wondrously bright smile sail swiftly back across her face.

"So that's what the bra is about. Sorry but I couldn't think of a gentler way to ask," finished Tadhg.

"Hmm, either that's the best chat up line I've ever heard or you're telling the truth," she said with a grin.

"Truth. Swear to God."

They both turned their heads to the bar as all at once the tunes started up again. Rosie was as curious as the devil.

"That is some story alright. We'll go in for a minute and then see what happens ok?"

"Yes no bother. I need a pint anyway. I've never told anyone half that stuff."

They went in together to see the two teams mingled around the table. Mick and the boys were playing away.

"Alright Rosie," said O'Malaigh.

"Well how's it going? Ye survived this length then?" she replied.

The table was quickly decorated with a round of drinks and the small talk so rudely interrupted in In Nomine Patri et Fili began again.

The music continued to dance around them and the craic was mighty. Ogee and O'Malaigh had made inroads and shoulders and elbows began to soften.

Gotta go, thought Tadhg.

The lads were in full flow and he'd explain all later.

"Mick, can I borrow you for a minute?"

Mick nodded. He knew it was time.

He tapped Eugene on the shoulder.

"Will ye come with me father?"

"Surely Tadhg," replied the priest and stood up.

"Here Pete, can you come too?"

"Fuck sake. If I have to?" he groaned mockingly.

"And Rosie…if you're still ok for the loan of…" began Tadhg.

"I've plenty more," she smiled.

As soon as they were outside Tadhg asked Mick for the fiddle which he duly handed over.

"Was there anywhere special here mum went? You know, with me? Kinda feels right to ask, ye know?"

"Of course Tadhg. There's a pretty special place for us all down here to be fair. She often took you."

"Aye? Where's that?"

"The beacon. 'Tis about a five minute walk."

"Back in a second," said Pete and lumbered quickly toward the car. He returned with a six pack of Harp.

"Emergency walk rations," he laughed and handed them out.

The five walked briskly along the sea front exchanging wee stories and yarns and soon were within sight of the beacon, the last great white stone memory of Ireland. They walked the stony grassy ground that dipped and rose under their toes until they stood in its emotional shadow.

"Next stop New York," said Mick.

There were no words for a moment. Tadhg thought of those whose last view of Ireland this was and cursed the banks for friends that were recently gone to find work. He missed them.

"Emm, if ye don't mind Rosie…"

She took herself off out of sight to the far side of the beacon and as quick was back.

Takes me bloody ages to get a bra off, thought Tadhg.

"Here ye go," she said and offered the holder of wonders.

"Don't stop there," blurted Pete.

"Settle big lad," she fired back.

"Shut up ye dose," laughed Tadhg.

Mick breathed slowly. It had been a while since he'd seen this action.

Tadhg quickly pulled the supporting wire out of the material and formed a little hook. He handed the lob-sided garment back to Rosie who quickly put it into her trouser pocket.

"Here goes…" said Tadhg.

Tadhg pushed the hook into the fiddle through the finely carved 'f' hole and tried to get some purchase on the sound post. After a couple of goes it had a good grip and he pulled it gently. He felt like a heart surgeon. After much gentle persuasion it fell, caught in the hook of the wire. He twisted his wrists, moved the fiddle and bent over nearly double until there it was, his past and future cocooned in this slightest piece of wood. He held the sound post up to the light and immediately saw the bottom was missing. The dowel was hollow and contained therein a rolled up piece of paper. All eyes leaned in closer and closer. He used the little hook again and pulled out the tiny passenger.

"Here Mick," he said and handed back the fiddle.

He slowly unfurled the paper and became aware of lines and dots all over one side. There was writing on the other.

"Ha, it's a tune. The Bank of Ireland," he laughed.

"Good tune," said Rosie.

"What does it say, Tadhg?" asked Pete.

My dearest Tadhg,
You did it! You found me again. With any luck you're reading this in the company of Mick, your father and Pete. I hope to God you're well and you've had a safe journey. This is a wee parting gift to you son. It's not much I suppose these days but it was all earned. Spend it how you will and know that I loved you every second of my life. Perhaps we'll talk about it all someday,

Le grá go deo (with love forever)
Mum

PS I hope you liked the tune, the account number is 31051978. (Your birthday!).

61. Session

"Thanks mum," said Tadhg.

"Ha, she was some blade, your Ma," said Mick. "The bank will be open at 9.30 tomorrow morning. I know the manager too, he was playing the fiddle beside me earlier."

Fuck, as long as they're not expecting me at opening time.

"I always knew she was clean mad," laughed Pete. "That's cousins for ye."

"God aye, we're related," laughed Tadhg.

"Fuck up ye wee shite or I'll knock yer bollox in," said Pete.

"Ah Maggie, Maggie …" sighed Eugene. "What a wonderful thing to do."

"Thanks Rosie. Couldn't have done without ye," said Tadhg.

"Oh you're quite a resourceful fella. Ye'd a got there," replied Rosie and took a long swallow from her tin.

Tadhg wanted to jump her bones right there.

"Tunes?" she said.

"Fuck yea," said Tadhg.

They were back into the bar in no time. The session had swelled to include the lads and lassies. Eugene and Pete headed straight for the bar. They had much to talk about. Tadhg and Rosie were delighted to see a couple of chairs kept free for them close to Mick's seat. It was like getting the Red Sea parted having a seat in there.

Tadhg ordered pints for himself and Rosie and soon had instruments at the ready. Mick left the old fiddle behind the bar.

"She's there for ye Tadhg," he said.

He had a spare one anyway which he also kept behind the bar.

Tadhg noticed Eugene shake hands with a young and much too healthily tanned man with a guitar case.

Hmm wonder what the story is there? Could be me fuckin' brother.

The evening sun shone in on the room which seemed to come alive as one large musical creature. Mick picked up the bow and launched himself into a reel to as many whoops and cheers as would do any goal or point.

The Gooseberry Bush, thought Tadhg. *He means business now.*

Like birds on the wing each of the musicians took off into their playing at a slightly different moment until the flock was circling and swooping among the pint glasses which soaked in the power of it. Indeed many began to vibrate toward the edge of their tables such was the foot tapping ferocity. It was as if the eternal energy of the very sea itself had somehow been channelled into the bar. Hands shot out just in time to prevent carnage.

Tadhg took a moment to look about. If there was an end to a rainbow to be chosen he'd forego the crock of gold for this; the craic, the music and sheer bloody enjoyment of it all. And to top the list was the definite potential of a court with the boul' Rosie.

Is there anything sexier than a girl playin' trad?

He knew there wasn't. He allowed himself a small smile and then a large gulp of the black promise in his hand.

He headed to the bar after a time to see the Pockel and the priest in conversation.

"Well Tadhg," said Eugene, "quite a day, eh?"

"Gonna be quite a tomorrow too," said Pete.

Eugene wasn't sure what tomorrow would bring. The last few days had asked him some very serious questions about his life and those clocks. Could he go back to such calm?

"Well Father, you heading north soon then?" asked Tadhg.

"Now Tadhg there's a question. All I'll say is I'm staying here tonight and I'm gonna make the most of it."

He raised his glass.

"To Maggie…and those that ever loved her."

"To Maggie."

The three clinked glasses.

"S'pose ye never know what's comin'…" said Eugene, in a too priestly manner for Pete.

"Well you do if you order three pints of Guinness."

"Ha, yes indeed. Do you think I could use that in my next sermon?"

"No better man," laughed Pete.

Ogee dandered up to join them.

"Sorted Tadhg?"

"Aye, dead on."

"I'm hearing talk of gigs goin' on the continent. Switzerland I think," he continued. "Just need someone to round up a few decent musos. Ye game?"

"Tour! With you fuckers?"

Might work. Be some craic.

"I have only one thing to say on the matter – "

He looked at Pete, who just knew…

"Pint."

Epilogue

Dear Mum,

Well what can I say? I'm sitting here with an outrageous hangover in the depths of West Cork waiting for a pint. The cure of course, just the one! Met a girl, Rosie, class looking and a laugh. She loves the tunes too, win-win. You were right about Pete, he's sound (got a wee issue with the fourth pint), good singer too. He drove us the length of the country over the last few days, near got us killed.

I'm going to meet up with Eugene later. I'm not sure how that'll all play out to be honest. He's a priest. You can pick them, Jesus!

Thanks for the money. I'm going to put it to good use...probably. Anyway the lads will be here soon enough, there may be tunes. Turns out Ogee knows a tour organiser in Germany. Long story short, looks like we're all hitting the road in the summer. The Germans still love the trad so I'm going to give the music a go for real. Yes I know, practising and a bit of graft. Sure we might do some recording too.

Mum, I'll write again soon (like it's not weird to write to your dead Ma)! We would have had some craic me and you...

Love
Tadhg